our
t
long
atter.
ark
et it
you,'
r,
urse

I'm to give it back to her t…
me wear her bead ring all the…
those pearl beads off the old pi…
make myself a ring? And oh, Mar…
that Mi… McPherson told her t…
Andr… Gillis that I had a…
…he first compliment I h…
…t imagine what a…
…a pret…
…se? I know…
… is well enough," said Marilla sh…
…s nose was a remarkable pr…
…f telling her so. That was three weeks
…ad go… …hly so far. And now, this crisp
…orning, An… …d Diana were tripping blithely
…rch Path, two of… …appiest little girls i…
"I guess Gilbert Blythe will be in school today," said

'It is the same thing with you,' said the…
tion dropped, and the party sat silent for…
thought over all she could remember abo…
which wasn't much. The Hatter was the fir…
'What day of the month is it?' he said, turn…
taken his watch out of his pocket, and was l…
shaking it every now and then, and holding i…
ered…
'Tw…
the…
best butter,' the March Ha…
'Yes, but some crumbs must have got in as well,'…
grumbled: 'you shouldn't have put it in with the bre…
March Hare took the watch and looked at it gloomily…
it into his cup of tea, and looked at it again: but he c…

Once on a dark winter's day,
heavy in the streets of Londo…
shop windows blazed with…
little girl sat in a cab with…
through the big thoroug…
She sat with her fee…
father, who held her…
the passing people…
big eyes. She was…
such a look on h…
child of twelve…
however, that…
could not he…
thinking th…

dreaming and thinking odd things and could not herself re…
time when she had not been thinking things about grown-up… long, lo…
…world they belonged to. She felt as if she had lived a long,…
…is moment she was remembering the voyage she had just mad…
…with her father, Captain Crewe. She was thinking of the big s…
…rs passing silently to and fro on it, of the children playing…
…ot deck, and of some young officers' wives who used t…
…lk to them and laugh at the things she said. Princi…
…what a queer thing it was that at one time one w…
…; and then in the middle of the ocean, and then…
…e through strange streets where the day w…
…this so puzzling that she moved…
…mysterious little voice…
…ing," Captain C…
face…

e replied…
e same year for s…
the case with mine,' said the…
eadfully puzzled. The Hatter's rema…
ave no sort of meaning in it, and yet it w…
nglish. 'I don't quite understand you,' she
olitely as she could.
ormouse is asleep again,' said the Hatter, and
ured a little hot tea upon its nose.
Dormouse shook its head impatiently, and said,
hout opening its eyes, 'Of course, of course; just
at I was going to remark myself.'
'Have you guessed the riddle yet?' the Hatter said,
turning to Alice again.
'No, I give it up,' Alice replied: 'what's the answer?'
'I haven't the slightest idea,' said the Hatter.
…said the March Hare.
'No… wearily. 'I think you might do something
…e,' she said, 'than waste it in asking
…wers.'
…as I do,' said the Hatter,
…it. It's him.' 'I don't
…course you do…

Once on a dark winter's day, when the yellow fog hung so
in the streets of London that the lamps were lighted and th…
blazed with gas as they do at night, an odd-looking little g…
with her father …nd was driven rather slowly through the b…
She sat with … tucked under her, and leaned agains…
held her … as she stared out of the window at th…
with a qu… …ashioned thoughtfulness in … big eye…
little girl that …e did not expect to s… …k on h…
would have been an old look for a ch… …and
seven. The fact was, however, that sh… …drea…
odd things and could not herself reme… …e w…
thinking things about grown-up people… …ld
felt as if she had lived a long, long time. At this mome…
ing the voyage she had just made from Bombay with…
Crewe. She was thinking of the big ship, of the Lasca…
and fro on it, of the children playing about on the h…
young officers' wives who used to try to make her t…
the things she said. Principally, she was thinking of…
that at one time one was in India in the blazing su…
of the ocean, and then driving in a strange vehicle…
where the day was as dark as the night. She foun…

"Indeed I was," said Anne comfortably. "It
wasn't so hard as you might imagine, either.
I sit with Diana. Our seat is right by the
window and we can look down to the Lake
of Shining Waters. There are a lot of nice
girls in school and we had scrumptious fun
playing at dinnertime. It's so nice to have a
lot of little girls to play with. But of course I
like Diana best and always will. I adore
Diana. I'm dreadfully far behind the
others. They're all in the fift…
only in the f…

ANNA JAMES

ILLUSTRATED BY
PAOLA ESCOBAR

PHILOMEL BOOKS

PHILOMEL BOOKS
An imprint of Penguin Random House LLC, New York

First published in the United States of America by Philomel Books,
an imprint of Penguin Random House, LLC, 2019.
First published in Great Britain by HarperCollins Children's Books in 2018.

Philomel Books is a registered trademark of Penguin Random House LLC.
Visit us online at penguinrandomhouse.com
Library of Congress Cataloguing-in-Publication Data is available upon request.
Printed in the United States of America
ISBN 9781984837127
1 3 5 6 7 9 10 8 6 4 2
Edited by Cheryl Eissing.
Design by Ellice M. Lee.
Text set in Adobe Caslon.

For my sister Hester,

who is made of the same stories as me

1

The View from the Gate of a Fairground

Matilda Pages pushed open the door of Pages & Co. and breathed in deeply, taking in the familiar scent of just-blown-out candles, dark chocolate, and, of course, books. For a second she forgot that she was splattered with muddy water and simply relished the week's holiday that stretched out in front of her like the view from the gate of a fairground. But the bubble of calm popped as the damp seeped through her tights, making her shiver, and she marched through the door connecting the bookshop to the narrow house she lived in with her grandparents. She let the door crash behind her, tossed her school bag on the table—accidentally sending a pile of potatoes flying—and flopped dramatically into a chair.

She paused, waiting for her grandmother to react, and when Grandma finally turned, Tilly flung her head theatrically onto her arms on the table.

"Happy half-term, Tilly," Grandma said, looking around in confusion. "What on earth is the matter? And why are you taking it out on the potatoes?"

Tilly's cheeks, usually fair with a smattering of freckles, blushed a deep raspberry as she sheepishly started picking up the potatoes.

"And you're soaking—it's not still raining, is it?" Grandma said, peering out of the kitchen window. She gave her granddaughter's head an affectionate rub as Tilly kneeled to rescue a stray potato that had rolled into the cat basket. Tilly sighed and leaned against Grandma's legs.

"Grace went through a puddle on her bike and it splashed all over me."

"Surely she didn't do it on purpose?" Grandma asked gently.

Tilly harrumphed in disagreement.

"Aren't you two as thick as thieves?" Grandma said.

"That was before, when we were just little. She has new friends now," Tilly said. "She got onto the netball team, and only wants to be with those girls now. She sits with Ammara and Poppy every day."

"Have I met Ammara and Poppy?" Grandma asked.

"No, they went to St. Enid's, and they stick together all the time."

"Well, why don't you invite some of them round during the holiday?" Grandma suggested. "Get to know each other?"

"I don't think they'd come," Tilly said uncertainly. "They're always whispering and giggling about something when I try to talk to them."

"They might surprise you. You don't know if you don't ask," Grandma said. "Be brave, Matilda. Be brave, be—"

"Be brave, be curious, be kind," Tilly interrupted. "I know."

"It's what we always used to tell your mum growing up," Grandma said.

"I just think being brave comes more naturally to some people than others," Tilly said.

"Often it's the things that don't come naturally to us that are the most important," Grandma said. "Now, why don't you take off that wet uniform and have a shower? I'll make you a hot chocolate to celebrate the start of the holidays."

Twenty minutes later Tilly was clean and dry, her dark brown curls considerably less damp, wearing her own clothes, carrying two mugs of hot chocolate covered in whipped cream, one for her and one for her grandad. She pushed the kitchen door open with her back and reversed into the bookshop. Pages & Co. was Tilly's favorite place in the world. From outside, on the busy north London high street, it looked like an entirely normal bookshop, but once inside it didn't quite make sense how everything fit inside its ordinary walls.

The shop was made up of five floors of corners and cubbyholes, sofas and squashy armchairs, and a labyrinth of bookshelves heading off in different directions. A spiral staircase danced up one wall, and painted wooden ladders stretched up into difficult-to-reach corners. Tall arched windows made it feel a little like a church when the light spilled in and dust motes danced in the air. When it was good weather the sun pooled on the floor and the bookshop cat—named Alice for her curious nature—could often be found dozing in the warmest spots. During the summer the big fireplace behind the till was filled to bursting with fresh flowers, but as it was October a fire was roaring there.

Tilly had never been very far outside London, but she felt like a seasoned traveler within the pages of books: she had raced across the rooftops of Paris, learned to ride a broomstick, and seen the northern lights from the deck of a ship. She had explored wonderlands and secret gardens with girls curious and contrary. She found books that led to long debates with Grandad over crumpets dripping with butter, and discovered stories that she read again and again until they shone far more brightly than the endless tests at school. She found friendships that seemed free of the complicated social rules at school. Tilly sometimes felt like there had been a lesson where friendship had been explained, but she'd been out sick and had never quite been able to catch up.

Grandad was behind the till, sorting through books that customers had ordered, matching receipts to titles and stacking them neatly, ready for collection. Tilly deposited the second mug of hot chocolate on the till, managing to avoid spilling most of it.

"Happy holidays, Tilly!" he said, clinking mugs with her. Grandad drank deeply and pretended, as he always did, that he didn't know he had whipped cream on his top lip. "Got much homework?"

"I have to read a book I've never read before," Tilly said, straight-faced.

"Goodness, sweetheart," Grandad said with a grin. "You'd better crack on with that immediately, if you even have a hope of finishing in a week."

Tilly giggled as she stuck a finger in her whipped cream, thinking of the pile of five books she had stacked next to her bed for her holiday reading.

"Ms. Webber did say that after the holidays we'd be starting a project about our favorite characters from books, and that if we wanted to get a head start on that we should think about who ours were. Who would you pick?"

"What a question," Grandad said, licking the cream from his lip. "I must admit my gut instinct is pulling me toward Sherlock Holmes, but I'll have to have a proper think and get back to you with my official answer. Now, other than your particularly arduous workload, what else do you have planned for the week? Is Grace coming over?"

"I don't know why you and Grandma keep asking me about Grace," Tilly said.

"Do we?" Grandad said, surprised. "Well, I thought she was your best friend?"

"I don't have a best friend," Tilly said firmly. "I've realized there isn't anyone who's best-friend material at school."

"And what exactly makes someone best-friend material?" Grandad asked.

"Someone who sticks by you; someone who never gets bored of talking to you. Someone who's adventurous, and clever, and brave, and funny . . ." Tilly said, checking her criteria off on her fingers. "Someone like Anne Shirley or Alice from Wonderland—those are *my* favorite characters, incidentally." With very few exceptions Tilly found that she much preferred the company of characters in her books to most of the people she knew in real life.

"I'm not sure best friends are a one-size-fits-all sort of situation, Tilly," Grandad said carefully. "Sometimes a person who becomes a friend is the least likely person you'd expect. Friends should bring out the best in you, not be the same as you. I'm sure you're someone's perfect fit."

Tilly tried to imagine herself as the perfect fit for a potential best friend. But when she thought about herself too directly she felt sort of fuzzy round the edges, like a photograph that was blurred, and when she compared herself to the characters she met in books their ink and paper felt more real than her bones and skin.

"And, for now, you've always got me," Grandad continued. "If you're in the market for an elderly best friend with whiskers and a bookshop."

"Exactly," Tilly said, trying to erase all thoughts of hypothetical best friends from her mind. "I don't need anyone who doesn't live in Pages & Co."

2

No One Has Proper Adventures in Real Life

The next morning Tilly woke up to the sound of rain and falling autumn leaves on her sloped skylight window. Rain meant quiet days in the shop as people stayed inside with only the odd group of bedraggled readers drying out in the café area, waiting for gaps in the downpour. She relished the school holidays with the familiar rhythms and rituals of the bookshop, and she savored every moment of her first-day-of-the-holidays routine: a chapter of a new book in bed while everything was quiet, getting dressed in anything that wasn't a school uniform, a lazy breakfast of one of Grandad's perfectly boiled eggs with toast soldiers.

"So, what's the plan for today?" Grandma asked, handing Tilly a mug of milky tea.

"Reading, mainly," Tilly said.

"Do you want to wander down to the woods with me

later?" Grandad suggested. "Or I need to pop in to the florist's and confirm all the flowers for the Wonderland party on Wednesday night—I could do with your eye for color. We've created a monster with this party, I sometimes think. Every year the customers and publishing folk seem to expect a more extravagant theme."

Tilly shrugged.

"Do you ever wish," she said, ignoring Grandad's question and turning to her grandparents with a serious look on her face, "that you had a relatively good friend in mortal peril that you could go and rescue?"

"I can't say that's something I spend much time thinking about," Grandma said, exchanging a look with Grandad across the table.

Tilly sighed. "I just wish there was something more exciting to do than go to the florist's," she said. "No one has *proper* adventures in real life."

"If I didn't want to get myself into hot water, I would say that someone who can't find adventure in the woods is lacking in imagination," Grandad said.

"You know what I mean."

"I do, my dear, but it never hurts to keep a weather eye open for adventures, even small ones."

"But for now," Grandma said, "why don't you stick with an adventure in a book, and if the rain ever stops, we can head out for a wander later."

Tilly opened the door into the bookshop and went to find Jack, who looked after the snug café area that took up a corner of the ground floor. When she reached the mismatched collection of chairs and tables he was nowhere to be found, so she went to see if there were any cakes she could sample, but, just as she reached out for a gooey-looking chocolate brownie, Jack's head popped over the counter.

"Aha! Caught red-handed!" he said.

"I was just looking," Tilly said sheepishly, before registering the wide smile on his face. "Why do you have honey on your forehead?" she asked.

"I'm experimenting with pop cakes," he said, holding up an ice-cube tray filled with sticky honey. "Remember in the Faraway Tree books by Enid Blyton? They eat those cakes that explode with honey when you bite into them? I'm going to freeze the honey so I can bake it in the middle of cupcakes. At least that's the plan—the honey is proving a little, well, uncooperative."

Jack, who was nineteen and saving up to go to pastry school in Paris, took his role as a bookshop baker very seriously and was always trying to re-create cakes and bakes from books. Tilly was under strict instructions to tell him whenever she came across a particularly tasty-sounding dish in a book she was reading. She had a suspicion he was using some of the new cookbooks for inspiration as well, as every once in a while she'd had to wipe off a smear of icing from a spine sticking out from a shelf, as though it had been put back in a hurry.

"Do you want some hot chocolate?" Jack offered as he manhandled the ice-cube tray into the tiny freezer section of the café fridge. "I'll bring it up."

Tilly nodded and grinned and then headed to her favorite reading corner on the first floor. Ten minutes later Jack sat down next to her, carefully holding a tray with two steaming mugs—and two brownies—on it. "If your grandparents notice me giving you brownies so soon after breakfast, just claim it's a very important baking experiment for the party, okay?"

He nudged her arm. "What are you reading?"

Tilly showed him the book cover, which was blue and glittery.

"I've just started. It's about mermaids and pirates and the ocean. It's probably not your kind of thing."

"Well, actually, Miss Tilly, I'll have you know I have quite a penchant for books about pirates and the ocean," he said. "But I like all sorts, really. I can't resist books set in space, especially if they've got something weird going on, or a really good twist. And, if there's some kind of intelligent robot, even better. Especially if it turns out to be evil. I know I should know this by now, but what are your favorites?"

"My two favorite books are *Anne of Green Gables* and *Alice in Wonderland*," Tilly replied with a great deal of certainty. "Anne and Alice are my favorite characters."

"Why do you like them so much then?"

She paused. "For lots of reasons, but I like them best because they seem real even when I'm not reading about them."

"What do you mean by real?" Jack asked.

Tilly contemplated the question.

"Like, sometimes when I don't know what to do I think about what Anne would do, or I find myself wanting to tell Alice about something I learned, and it takes a second before I remember they're not real people I can just go and talk to."

Jack smiled. "Often characters in books are considerably more consistent than the people around us. All that messy life stuff does rather get in the way. Speaking of," he said, brushing crumbs off his apron as a tinny beep sounded through the shop, "my pop cakes are calling. Come and try one in a bit."

He pushed himself up from the squishy sofa and disappeared down the stairs, leaving Tilly to her book.

A little while later Tilly was interrupted from her adventures under the sea by the sound of her grandma's laughter tumbling down the stairs. Tilly couldn't remember the last time she'd heard Grandma laugh like that, or the last time she herself had laughed so hard either, so she tiptoed up the stairs to see what was causing it. She found Grandma tucked in a corner, wiping tears from her eyes as a woman with dark curly hair pinned up on the back of her head waved her hands around animatedly. She seemed quite a lot younger than Grandma and wore a long, old-fashioned-looking dress. Tilly crept closer, wanting to hear what Grandma was finding so funny, without interrupting the moment.

"And do you know, he turned to him and said in the most insufferable voice, 'She is tolerable, but not handsome enough to tempt me.' I tell you, Elsie, I held Charlotte's hand very tightly to stop myself going over and telling him exactly what I thought of his manners, especially when he was so new to town. Of course, my mother will forgive a man that rich almost anything, although this tested even her resolve."

No longer able to resist Grandma's giggles, Tilly coughed loudly and rounded the corner only to find Grandma sitting by herself.

"Oh, Tilly!" she said, still hiccuping a little. "Are you okay, darling?"

"Where's that woman gone?" Tilly asked, looking around in confusion, unable to understand how she'd left so quickly and quietly.

Grandma's laughter abruptly stopped. "Which woman, darling?" she asked, sitting up straighter.

"The woman you were just talking to, of course," Tilly said.

"The one with the long dress and the dark hair—the one who made you laugh like that!"

"Oh, her," Grandma said slowly. "That's Lizzy—she's an old friend. You caught a glimpse of her, did you?"

"She was literally just sitting here as I came up the stairs," Tilly said, confused. "Where's she gone?"

"She must have slipped past without you noticing. You know how this place is like a rabbit warren; it's impossible to keep track of everything and everyone. I'm forever losing you in here!" Grandma said, more composed. "Anyway! Enough of that! How's your book?"

Tilly had the distinct feeling that Grandma wasn't telling her something.

"How long have you known Lizzy for?" she asked, ignoring Grandma's question.

"Oh, a long time now."

"She's not very old, though?" Tilly persisted.

"No, I suppose she's not. But she's an old soul." Grandma smiled. "She's . . . well, Tilly, if I tell you the truth, part of the reason I enjoy spending time with her is that she reminds me of your mum, very much."

"Mum?" Tilly sat down on the now-empty chair opposite Grandma, hungry for details and feeling her heart punch against her rib cage. "What reminds you of her? She doesn't really look like her, does she?"

"No, not particularly," Grandma said. "It's more how she

holds herself, her sense of humor, her way of telling stories. Your mum used to make me laugh in the same way Lizzy does."

"Did my mum know her too? Were they friends? How old is Lizzy?" Tilly asked.

"Ah, a little older than she looks," Grandma said. "I first met Lizzy years before your mum left. I need to get her skincare secret, hey?"

Tilly was feeling light-headed with this new information about her mother, whom she'd only known as a baby. Beatrice Pages had left when Tilly was tiny, and Tilly had grown used to not speaking about her to avoid reopening old wounds that seemed to haunt Grandma and Grandad. Sometimes she lost her grandad for days at a time if she asked questions; he was physically there, but barely seemed to notice anything going on around him, ignoring customers and Tilly alike. So when these precious gems of information emerged Tilly gathered them to her and guarded them fiercely.

"Anyway, that's enough chat about old friends," Grandma said, bringing the conversation to a close with a firm nod of her head. "Do you have a moment to come and help me in the stockroom?"

Tilly nodded, and Grandma took her hand as they walked down the stairs together, where they were immediately pounced on by a panicked-looking Jack.

"I need help!" he wailed.

"What's wrong?" Grandma asked, as Tilly imagined an array of horrible accidents involving honey, or knives, or both.

"I can't find the vanilla essence!" Jack shouted, making two people sitting drinking coffee eye him warily and Alice the cat raise her head in disdain from the cushioned seat she had claimed for the morning.

Grandma sighed.

"That's all?" Tilly said. "I thought you'd hurt yourself. I thought it was an emergency."

Jack looked surprised.

"This *is* an emergency. I need to get the vanilla in the batter now. Do you have any in the kitchen, Elsie, or could you go and ask Mary, Tilly?"

Grandma took a deep breath. "Tilly, you go and check the kitchen and see if you can find some in the pantry. I'm going to get back to the stock cupboard."

"Don't get honey on my book," Tilly said sternly, putting it behind the counter before heading to the kitchen.

There was nothing in the pantry so Tilly rifled through the kitchen cupboards, but she couldn't find any vanilla essence there either. The cupboards seemed to be full of everything and nothing all at the same time, the result of her grandad's inability to throw anything away in case it proved useful later, however much it looked like junk to Tilly and Grandma. She found one orange sock, several pencils, and the red half of a pack of cards, but no vanilla.

And then, tucked away behind a heap of empty shoeboxes, she found a dusty cardboard box wrapped in packing tape. On the top flap it had "Bea's Books" written in black marker. Tilly felt her heart squeeze and a crackle of something she couldn't identify deep inside her: these were her mum's stories.

3

Other People's Memories

Tilly dragged the box into the kitchen and peeled off the tape, which had turned crunchy with age. The noise of the bookshop melted away, and her hand drifted to the tiny gold bee necklace round her neck, a gift from her mother when Tilly was born, which matched the one Bea had worn herself.

Tilly's idea of her mum was stitched together from a patchwork of old photos and other people's memories. No one knew where Beatrice Pages had gone, and this lack of facts meant that the hole her mother had left had torn, ragged edges that were slow to knit back together.

Tilly had almost given up asking, but when she did, conversations about Bea's disappearance always went the same way.

"Love, we've told you everything we know, and what the police think. It's not good to dwell on what happened," one of her grandparents would say.

"But the police think she was unhappy and just left to start again somewhere. I don't understand why she would have done that just after I was born if she . . ." Tilly found it hard to voice the end of that thought.

The reassurances always came. "Tilly, she loved you very, very much. We know that without any doubt at all."

"I just don't understand why she would leave if she loved me so much." Tilly couldn't help but come back to the same question she always asked, feeling the prick of tears as she spoke.

"We don't understand either, Tilly, my love. We wish we did," Grandma would say, and Grandad, as always, would quietly wipe his eyes with his tartan handkerchief.

Tilly pulled her mind back to the box in front of her. Inside were piles of old books, the paper yellowing and the covers tattered and ripped. Tilly stared at them, not sure where to start, but as she went to pull out the top book she heard Jack calling from the shop.

"Tilly! Vanilla! I'm smearing honey on your book as I speak!"

The bubble popped, and Tilly sighed and pushed the box to the side of the kitchen. She wanted to save it until she had uninterrupted time to look through it properly, the way she made sure she had time to savor a new book.

She went back through to Jack in the bookshop. "I couldn't find any vanilla; you should ask Mary," Tilly said.

"Well, go on then." Jack gestured impatiently. "Go and ask her."

Tilly opened her mouth to make an excuse, wanting to return to the box of books. But the words weren't there, so she turned and grabbed an umbrella from by the door, but skidded on something squishy underfoot. She looked down to see a half-eaten sandwich on the wooden floor. She tutted to herself as she picked it up.

"Honestly, who eats marmalade sandwiches?" she said to herself as she threw it in the bin outside the shop, and crossed the road to Crumbs, the café run by Mary Roux.

Mary and Jack had a long-standing, mostly affectionate rivalry that was almost entirely one-sided. Mary was always lending Jack things he was missing, and offering him baking tips.

The bell above the door jangled as Tilly went in. She didn't spot Mary straightaway, but she saw Oskar, Mary's son, sitting at a table toward the back. He was writing or doodling in a notebook, a slice of toast abandoned to one side, and Tilly couldn't help but notice his brown skin had inky fingerprints on it. A moment later Mary's face appeared behind the counter. She was carrying a plate of cupcakes iced in pastel shades, which she handed to a couple with a happily gurgling baby.

Mary grinned when she saw Tilly and beckoned her over once the family had sat down.

"What can I help you with?" Mary asked. "Has Jack been experimenting again?"

"He's trying to make pop cakes, like the ones in the Enid Blyton books," Tilly explained, "but he's run out of vanilla and he wondered if he could have a little bit of yours, if you can spare some?"

"Of course, of course," Mary said. "Sit down. Let me grab some from the kitchen. Do you want some lunch while you wait? You look a bit peaky."

"I'm okay," Tilly said. She looked up at Mary, testing how she felt about sharing the news about the box with her. "I just found some of my mum's old stuff. It's put me in a bit of a funny mood, I guess. I don't have much that was hers."

"Oh, love. I can see why that might have thrown you," Mary said before planting a kiss on the top of Tilly's head. Her hand rested on Tilly's shoulder a little longer than it usually did and then Tilly felt a squeeze as Mary headed off toward the kitchen. "Sit down. I'll be right back."

As the door through to the kitchen swung shut, Tilly looked at Oskar and tried to make eye contact. He didn't ever seem to be in Crumbs when Tilly was there, and he'd gone to a different primary school, so although they shared some lessons now they'd never really spoken much.

She tried to wander over casually.

"Have you started your English homework yet?" she asked, and Oskar looked up.

"No?" Oskar said in surprise. "It's literally the first day of the holidays. But we have to read a book by an author we've never read before, right?"

"Yep," Tilly said happily. "Best homework ever."

"I was thinking . . . I might come and find something at Pages & Co. later. Maybe? If that was okay?" he asked.

Tilly beamed. "That's a great idea. I can help you find something, if you want? What do you like to read?"

Oskar scuffed his feet together and looked down at the table.

"All sorts. I started reading the first Percy Jackson book in the summer holidays and I'm really enjoying it."

"They're so good, right?" Tilly said. "I could not believe it when I found out who Nico's dad was."

"Don't tell me!" Oskar said. "I haven't got to that bit yet—I'm still on the first one. I read kind of slowly."

"Oskar's dyslexic," Mary said, coming up behind them, a small bottle in one hand and a brown envelope tucked under her arm. "But he still loves reading, don't you, my love?"

"All right, Mum," Oskar said, brushing his mum's hand off his head in embarrassment.

"Right, well, you should definitely come over to the shop for your homework book, though," Tilly said.

"Yes, thank you, Tilly. That would be lovely. Why don't you pop round now, Oskar?" Mary said, smiling widely.

"All right, Mum, chill out, okay?" Oskar said. He turned to Tilly. "I'll come round tomorrow?"

Tilly nodded.

"Oh, and here's the reason you came over," Mary said, holding out a tiny bottle of vanilla essence. "Could you let Jack know I don't need it back as long as I can try one of his pop cakes?" She grinned, before putting the envelope down on the table between them and pushing it toward Tilly, who looked at her quizzically.

"When you told me about your mum's books it made me think of this," she said slowly. "I've had it for ages. I should have given it to you sooner, but, well, when Bea left I tucked it away, and it just slipped my mind until you mentioned finding her things."

Neither Tilly, Mary, nor Oskar seemed sure what to say or do next, so Mary pulled the envelope back toward her and slid out a slightly faded photograph that showed Bea and Mary as young women on a sofa in the shop. They sat at either end, with their socked feet touching in the middle, and both of them had books resting on top of their heavily pregnant bellies. Mary's hair was in an afro, rather than the braids Tilly was used to seeing, and her own mum had long auburn hair spread over the back of the sofa.

"I'm sorry I haven't taken better care of it, Tilly," Mary said as she tried to rub away a smear from one corner of the picture. "But it's yours now, if you want it. I know it's only one photo, but I thought you might like it anyway. I can tell you a bit more about it, if you like, but I understand if you'd rather look properly by yourself first. I can picture that day perfectly. I haven't the foggiest what book I was reading, but your mum went on a real classics binge while she was pregnant, nostalgic for her own childhood, I suppose.

That book is *A Little Princess;* she read it over and over. It was her favorite—although I'm sure you know that. You can come and ask me about the photo or your mum anytime you like, you know."

"Thank you," Tilly said quietly, staring at the photo. That was the first time she'd heard *A Little Princess* was her mum's favorite book. Mary slid the picture back into the envelope and passed it to Tilly.

"Go on, get back to Jack, and make sure to bring me over a pop cake later." Mary gave her a gentle push toward the door. "And keep that envelope out of the rain."

After dropping the vanilla off with Jack, Tilly went back into the kitchen to find Grandad sitting on the floor, leaning against the wall next to the box with his hanky out. Tilly slid down the wall next to him and squeezed in under his arm, breathing in his familiar smell of cashmere jumpers and old paper.

"I'd forgotten where I'd put these," he said, hugging Tilly close to him. "They were some of your mum's books when she was your age. She'd been rereading a lot of them while she was pregnant with you."

"These were her favorites?" Tilly prompted, eager for more details.

"Yes, well, her favorites when she was growing up. These were ones that meant a lot to her when she was around your age. The books we love when we're growing up shape us in a special way, Tilly. The characters in the books we read help us decide who we want to be."

Grandad paused, and Tilly noticed he had a book in his hands, turning it round and round as he spoke.

"Ah. This one," he said. "I wasn't sure whether to show you. I mean . . . Well, just let me know what you think of it." He gave a last glance at the book in his hand and passed it to Tilly. It was *A Little Princess*—a copy with a yellow cover. Tilly took Mary's photo out of the envelope and showed it to Grandad.

"Where did you get this from?" he asked.

"Mary just gave it to me," Tilly said. "Look, she's reading this exact book!"

"You see, it was her favorite," Grandad said. "She enjoyed it when she was your age, but she really fell in love with it while she was at university. She took this copy with her and read it over and over again. She . . . well, she found something new in it as an adult, I suppose. Have you read it?"

"Yes, a few times."

"What did you think?" Grandad asked. "Did you connect with any characters in particular?"

Tilly shrugged. "I enjoyed it. It's not my favorite but I liked Sara a lot. I like how she tells stories when she feels sad, and to help her after her dad dies."

Grandad smiled softly, as much to himself as to Tilly. "Well, now you have your mum's copy to keep. And a photo of her reading it."

He looked at the box of books. "There might be some in there you haven't read before. Why don't you take them up to your room and have a sort through?" He gave Tilly a squeeze and hauled himself up off the floor. "Can't leave your grandma to deal with Jack by herself for too long," he said, and headed back into the bookshop.

Tilly put *A Little Princess* back in the box and staggered upstairs with it to her tiny room at the very top of the house. The walls were lined with bookshelves full of her own books, as well as ones she had temporarily borrowed from the shop, something she was not really supposed to do, but after she caught Grandma spilling tea on what turned out to be a shop book a blind eye was usually turned as long as they reappeared in pristine condition. Tilly put the box down in the middle of the floor and placed Mary's envelope on top. She sat down on her bed, curled her knees up underneath her, and stared at them as her feelings tangled round each other, twisting and knotting her up.

Finally she pulled the photo out again and laid it on her bed before slipping a narrow album off her shelves. In the pages were a collection of photos her grandparents had let her collate that all featured her mum: as a child, with Grandma and Grandad, in the bookshop, even some in New York, where she had gone to university. The photos looked back at Tilly, a puddle of memories that weren't hers.

Tilly felt like she was being wrapped in a heavy blanket

that was comforting and suffocating at the same time. Her mum's face looked up at her from too many photos all at once. When Tilly tried to picture her mum in her mind she felt like she was trying to imagine what a character in a book looks like. You think they're standing right next to you, but as soon as you whirl round to look straight at them everything blurs and dissolves, and the harder you try to see them, the more flighty and unfocused they get until they barely resemble a real person at all.

She tried to calm her breathing down and tucked Mary's photo into the album, before putting it on her bedside table. Then she took a deep breath and settled down to look at the box of books instead, which felt more manageable.

"Books are my thing," she muttered to herself. "I can do books."

She tried to blow the dust off the top of the box, but it worked rather less well than it did in films, so she wiped it with her sleeve. There wasn't any other writing on the box apart from her mum's name in blocky capitals. Tilly peeled back the rest of the barely sticky tape and pulled out the copy of *A Little Princess*. Underneath that was a dated-looking version of *Anne of Green Gables*, which she picked up, but she found herself just gazing at the cover, unable to open it. The top front corner was ripped off and she could see "Beatrice Pages" written on the first page in a child's handwriting.

Tilly traced the lines of her mother's writing with a fingertip, trying to picture her mum at her age carefully inking a little bit of herself onto the paper. Tilly felt as though there was a delicate thread stretched between her and her mother that she had only realized was there when this book had tugged on it. Grandad had always told her to write her name in her books, so it shouldn't have come as a surprise that her mum did the same thing when she was little.

"It's about creating a record of who's read and loved each book," he would say. Grandad was always hunting in charity shops for copies that had someone's name in, or messages from people who had given books as presents. "I love thinking about other people reading the books I love, or why someone gave that book as a present—those names and messages are like tiny moments of time travel linking readers from different eras and families and even countries."

Tilly wondered why her mother had cared for these books, for they were clearly very well loved. Tilly wanted to know if her mother had loved these characters for the same reasons she did. Had Anne Shirley made her mum laugh in the same places? She closed her eyes and imagined a parallel life where she could ask her, where she could go downstairs and find her at the kitchen table, chopping salad leaves with Grandad, or rubbing flour and butter together to make crumble topping with Grandma. Their house was always full of laughter and music and conversation, but Tilly could hear the silence where her mother should be, like an orchestra without a cello section.

She was pulled from her imagination by a gentle knock on the door, and Grandma popped her head round.

"Hi, sweetheart, how are you getting on? Grandad said you'd found a box of your mum's books?"

Tilly nodded as Grandma stepped into the room and picked up the copy of *A Little Princess*. She held it to her chest like it contained a small part of her daughter in its pages. "I'm going to start thinking about dinner soon," she said, still hugging the book tightly. "Do you want to come down and help close the shop up beforehand? It's a bit chilly up here."

Tilly nodded and followed Grandma downstairs. And, even though she knew the kitchen would be empty, she couldn't help but picture opening the door to her mother. But as she went in and felt the warmth of the room envelop her she rooted herself once again in the present.

Later that evening, over a meal of chicken roasted with garlic and lemons and rosemary, with crusty bread and green beans, Tilly felt the hard gem of her sadness thaw a little, leaving questions as it melted.

"Do you know what sort of books my dad liked?" she asked, and Grandad seemed to choke a little on a mouthful of bread.

"I'm afraid not," Grandma said as she patted Grandad on the back. "We didn't really know him very well at all."

"Do you think my mum would have known his favorite books?" Tilly asked.

"I'm sure she did," Grandma said. "I'm sure they talked

about books along with everything else you talk to the person you love about."

"Why don't we have any photos of him?"

"Well, for the same reason that we don't know what his favorite books were: we just didn't get to spend any time with him before he died."

"Do you think Mum left because my dad died?"

"Oh, my love," Grandma said. "'I don't know' is the honest answer. I'm not going to pretend to you that it didn't break her heart not being able to be with your father for longer, or that she didn't spend a lot of time thinking about how things might have worked out differently. But then she had you, and she had a little bit of him back again, and that's part of the reason you were so precious to her."

"I wonder which bits of me are from him?" Tilly said.

Grandad smiled. "Well, you didn't get your hair or your height from us. Although I have a sneaking suspicion that you might have inherited your literary tastes from our side of the family."

"But, Tilly," Grandma said, "you may have a bit of him and a bit of her and a bit of us all mixed in there, but the best bits of you are all your own, that much I know. Now. Whose turn is it to do the washing-up?"

When Tilly had been small she had read with Grandad every night before she went to bed. Every evening after dinner, Tilly and Grandad would curl up on the big, squishy sofa in front of the fireplace, and Grandad would read aloud a chapter or two of whichever book they were engrossed in. Together they had gone sailing with the Swallows and Amazons, met the witches of Miss Cackle's Academy, and visited worlds balanced on the backs of elephants.

As Tilly got older the tradition had gradually faded; first they started reading their own books next to each other, exploring vast and separate worlds while sitting side by side, and then Tilly had started taking her books up to bed to read, and before she knew it, and without anyone making a particular decision about it, they didn't read together anymore.

Later that evening, with her mum's copy of *Anne of Green Gables* still closed, Tilly crawled out of bed and crept back downstairs. Her grandma was reading with a cup of tea at the kitchen table and looked up when Tilly came in. Seeing the book in Tilly's hand, she just smiled and went back to her own. Tilly pushed the door to the shop open and saw Grandad on the sofa, lit up by the flickering light of the fire. She crawled up beside him and put her mum's copy of the book on his knee. Without saying anything he put his arm round her, and when Grandma came through with three mugs of hot chocolate he put his own book down and began to read.

4

Somewhere Adventures Live

The next morning Tilly was sitting at the kitchen table, reading her mum's copy of *Anne of Green Gables,* when Grandad popped his head round the bookshop door. He came and gave Grandma a kiss on the cheek as she simmered gooseberries on the stove, singing under her breath along with the radio.

"Oskar's here," he said to Tilly, smiling. "He said you'd promised to help him find a book."

"Oh, I didn't think he'd come," Tilly said, putting a bookmark carefully in her mum's book and placing it well out of reach of the sticky gooseberries. She headed into the shop and saw Oskar wandering between the bookshelves, trailing his fingertips along the spines of the books. Tilly watched him soak up the atmosphere of the shop for a moment.

"Have you never been here before?" she asked, making Oskar jump a little.

"I didn't hear you come in," he said sheepishly. "And yes, of course I've been in before; it's where Mum gets all her Christmas presents. But I'd forgotten how . . ." He paused.

"Magical?" Tilly suggested. "Exciting? Beautiful?"

"Yes, but that's not what I mean. It's not what it looks like, it's how it makes you feel, isn't it? Is there a word that means somewhere adventures live?"

"I don't think so, but there should be," Tilly said.

"But anyway," Oskar said, collecting himself, "it's cool, is what I mean. But I haven't been in for ages. I'm not up this way that much. We have someone else who looks after the café on weekends, and I usually spend the school holidays with my dad."

"Where does your dad live?"

"In Paris, with my big sister, Emilie."

"Oh wow, I thought you were going to say south London or something," Tilly said. "It must be amazing to get to spend the holidays there. I've never even been outside of England."

"Yeah, I guess," Oskar said. "Paris is pretty cool, but Dad got remarried last summer and Marguerite's really nice, but now it kind of feels like I'm visiting someone else's home when I'm there. And Emilie is always out with her friends, so I decided not to go this holiday."

"How come Emilie lives with your dad?" Tilly asked.

"She decided to go to college there," Oskar explained. "She wants to be fluent in French so she can get into university there too. Her boyfriend lives in Paris."

"Do you miss them?" Tilly asked.

"Yeah, I guess. I don't know. I miss my sister more than my dad, I think. Sometimes it feels like I'm in the way when I'm there. Not that I'm not wanted, but that it would be easier if I weren't there." Oskar paused. "Do you miss your parents?" he asked quietly, as though he wasn't sure if he was allowed to talk about them.

"Mostly it's almost fine," said Tilly, surprising herself at how comfortable she felt talking to Oskar honestly, "but every so often I can feel the gap where they should be. It's not like that all the time, but I'm always aware of it a little bit."

"What happened to them?" Oskar asked, still looking at his feet.

"My dad got ill and died. I don't know many of the details. He had to go abroad for work; he got ill; he died before he could get home. We don't really know what happened to my mum. She left really soon after I was born without telling Grandma and Grandad or anyone where she was going, and she never came back. We haven't heard from her since."

"Whoa, that's like something from a TV show," Oskar said, before stopping. "I'm sorry. I didn't mean . . . It must be horrible. Do you really not know anything?"

Tilly shrugged. "She didn't leave a note or anything. The police think that maybe she had postpartum depression and she ran away and is living a completely new life somewhere else. They said she might try to make contact at some point, but that I shouldn't get my hopes up."

"Do you think about your parents a lot?"

"Kind of. It's funny because I can't remember them at all, so it's hard to miss them or feel sad about them in a very specific way. It's like feeling sad that you never had a diamond ring, or a unicorn. I feel sad about the idea of them, and knowing that they're not here, and I hate that I don't understand why Mum left—but I don't really have any memories of them as real people. I have this, though." Tilly pulled out her necklace from under her jumper and showed Oskar. The small gold bee was no bigger than the nail on Tilly's thumb.

"Was that your mum's?" Oskar asked.

"No, it's mine but she had one just the same. Hers was a present from my dad and when I was born she had one made for me too." Tilly tucked it back into her jumper.

The shop phone suddenly started ringing and made them both jump.

"Anyway, I've never really told anyone else about all of that," Tilly said a little awkwardly.

"I'm glad—" Oskar started, but Tilly cut him off.

"Let's find a book for English. I need a new one too."

Oskar nodded and followed her up the stairs to the children's floor. Tilly picked out a pile of books for Oskar that she knew were printed on a different kind of paper that made it easier for people with dyslexia to read and placed them in front of him with a flourish.

While Oskar flicked through them, she went to find *A*

Little Princess and realized the shop stocked several different editions. She looked through some of the different covers, wishing she'd had the chance to talk to her mum about the book. She was sliding the various editions back onto the shelf when, after careful consideration, Oskar settled on a slim book with a black cover and a creepy illustration on the front.

They took it downstairs, where Grandad put it in a canvas tote bag stamped with the Pages & Co. logo and refused to let Oskar pay for it.

"It's a pleasure to have you in Pages & Co.," Grandad said. "Special offer for friends of the shop."

Oskar thanked Grandad and gave Tilly an awkward half-wave before making his way back across the road to Crumbs.

Tilly headed upstairs to her reading nook, but when she turned the corner she saw that her sofa was already occupied by a girl with red pigtails. She looked up at Tilly as she approached and sighed dramatically.

"I know what you must be thinking," she said in an accent that Tilly couldn't place. "You're thinking what a dreadful burden it must be for a girl who is already so skinny to be forced to endure red hair as well."

"I wasn't thinking that at all," Tilly said. "I was just wondering what you were doing on my sofa?"

"I'm so awfully sorry," the girl said, jumping up and haphazardly straightening the cushions, "I didn't know it was yours."

"I mean, it's not really," Tilly said, realizing that she must have seemed rude. "It's just where I like to sit and read, and you surprised me. I hadn't noticed you when I was up here with my fri—with a boy from school."

"Oh, I know that feeling," the girl said, smiling broadly. "I have a tree that is laden with the most beautiful, sweet-smelling, pale pink blossoms that I like to read under." The girl's face suddenly morphed into a look of horror. "But can you ever forgive me?"

"Forgive you for what?" Tilly said, thoroughly flummoxed at the change in tone.

"My horrible manners. I haven't even introduced myself. My name is Anne. With an 'e.'"

"With an 'e'?" Tilly repeated hazily.

"Yes, the 'e' is ever so important. People are always telling me that the name is much the same with or without the 'e,' but I think those people are severely lacking in imagination. How could you ever think that Ann without an 'e' was the same as Anne with an 'e'? It's like saying . . . Why, it's like saying that dessert is the same as desert! But there I go again with my terrible manners. I haven't even asked what your name is. Oh, wait! Let me guess, you look like . . . an Emmeline, or maybe a Penelope. Or Cordelia?" she added, sounding hopeful.

"It's just Tilly, I'm afraid. Short for Matilda, Matilda Pages."

"Why, that is a lovely name and I am quite envious," Anne said, looking entirely delighted. "I'm so thrilled to meet you."

"Are you looking for a book?" Tilly asked.

"That sounds wonderful, thank you!" Anne said. "Autumn *is* the most magical time of the year for reading, don't you think?" She gestured toward the window, which framed only drizzle and gray skies, but Anne reacted as though she could see auburn leaves tumbling in the wind. "October is my absolute favorite month. And to read outside, with the sun dappling . . . Do you think dappling is a real word, Tilly? I think it must be, don't you? With the sun dappling the leaves of a tree, a glass of raspberry cordial at hand . . ." She tailed off, staring dreamily into nothing.

Tilly began to find the silence a little awkward, but struggled to think of something to say and so returned to her fail-safe question. "What's your favorite story?" she asked, jerking Anne out of her autumnal daydreams.

"Do stories you've made up yourself count?" asked Anne.

"I don't think so," said Tilly. "I think they have to be, well, proper stories, like in a book."

"A story you've made up yourself is just as proper, don't you think? Although I suppose it is harder to share with other people unless it's written down. But I do love telling stories out loud as well. My friend Diana and I have a club where we read each other our stories and offer helpful advice on how to improve as writers. I must say, though, the advice is mainly one-way. Poor Diana, she doesn't have much of an imagination, although I love her fiercely regardless. I daresay it is good for my soul to be bosom friends with a girl who is so lacking in imaginative powers."

The mention of a friend named Diana made Tilly's brain itch; something about this girl was so familiar.

"But, anyway, it must depend on what the purpose of your story is, I suppose," Anne concluded, and looked up triumphantly.

Tilly nodded supportively, although she wasn't really very sure what Anne's point was.

"Do you know," Tilly started, glancing down at the book in her hand, "you do remind me of—" But she was interrupted by a harried-looking man who came up behind them and tapped Tilly on the shoulder imperiously.

"Excuse me, young lady, I need to pay for this immediately. Do you work here?" He was holding a very thick business textbook.

"Not really," Tilly said, trying not to laugh as Anne impersonated the man's cross face behind his back. "But I'll go and find my grandad. He owns the shop."

The man nodded curtly.

"I'll be right back," Tilly said to Anne.

"I don't trust you to come straight back, missy. I'll come with you; I have an incredibly important meeting to get to urgently," the man said, and Tilly couldn't be bothered to explain that she wasn't talking to him. She delivered him to Grandad, who took him to the till, but when Tilly went back upstairs she couldn't see Anne anywhere. She ran down to find Grandad after the grumpy customer had gone.

"Ah, Tilly, just the person I was looking for. Don't forget, we need some of your inspiration for the Wonderland party later. I'd been wondering if we could possibly try to . . ." He paused, noticing how distracted she was. "What's up, sweetheart?"

"Did you see a girl come past here a few moments ago?" she asked.

"No, afraid not, love. Was she a friend from school?"

"No, just a customer, I think. She seemed nice, though. I thought she might have stuck around for a bit," Tilly said. "But I can't find her."

"She probably had to go and meet her parents, Tils," Grandad said gently. "Maybe she'll pop back in later. I'll keep an eye out for her if she comes in; what did she look like?"

"She had red hair in two plaits," Tilly said. "It was funny actually; she really reminded me of Anne Shirley from *Anne of Green Gables*—and her name was even Anne too! Such a weird coincidence. Maybe it's like owners and their dogs," she joked. "You start seeing your favorite characters in real people. Although that's not quite right with the dog thing, is it . . . ?" She tailed off, noticing Grandad's face had gone pale. "Are you okay? Should I get Grandma? Do you need a cup of tea?"

"No, no, I'm fine, love," Grandad reassured her. "Just a wobbly moment. Been on my feet for too long this morning, I think! I will take you up on that tea, though, and I'll just have a sit-down behind here for a moment—I'll be as right as rain before you know it." The color was already returning to his cheeks as Tilly left to make the tea.

5

Magic, Mischief, Nonsense

While the kettle boiled, Tilly seized the chance to run upstairs to her room and dig out her mum's copy of *Alice in Wonderland*, tucking Mary's photo inside the cover.

Grandad wasn't at the till when she returned with the tea. She tracked him down in the corner of the shop that they rather grandly called the office, although it was really just a desk tucked into a corner of the fourth floor where customers didn't venture as regularly. As she headed toward the office a sweet, smoky smell lingered in the air, one that got stronger as she got closer to the desk, alongside a murmur of voices. Someone very posh was responding languidly to Grandad's questions, and as Tilly rounded the corner she saw a tall, elegant man in an expensive-looking gray coat sitting opposite Grandad. To Tilly's surprise he was smoking a black pipe, which was the cause of the sweet scent in the air, and he was wearing an odd hat with a flap on each side, even though it was always cozy inside the shop.

"I don't mean to be rude but I don't think you should be smoking in here," she said, putting down Grandad's cup. The man and Grandad stopped talking abruptly and stared at her, before turning to look at each other.

"Sorry, I didn't mean to interrupt your meeting, Grandad," Tilly said, instantly worried she'd been too terse with someone who looked decidedly important. "I just wanted ask you something, but I'll come back later." Grandad nodded mutely and Tilly went back downstairs, but only a few moments later she heard her name being called.

"Tilly!" Grandad's voice came down the stairs. "Wait for me a sec, will you?" Tilly paused, so Grandad could catch up with her. "Sorry about that, love," he said, back to his usual self. "I was just deep in conversation and entirely forgot I'd asked for that cup of tea. Sorry if I was strange with you; you know how I get: can't concentrate on more than one thing at a time."

"It's okay," Tilly said. "Who was that anyway, and why were you letting him smoke?"

Grandad looked sheepish. "Ah, he's an old friend, and he likes doing things his way, so I let the rules slide for him and turn a blind eye. I know it's ill-advised."

"I can't seem to turn a corner in this place without interrupting someone else's conversation," Tilly said.

"What on earth do you mean, sweetheart?" Grandad said.

"I barged in on Grandma catching up with a friend yesterday too," Tilly said. "And that lady vanished as soon as I interrupted; I just seem to make everything awkward."

"Which lady was that?" Grandad asked slowly.

"I think she was called Lizzy," Tilly said. "Grandma said she reminded her of Mum."

Grandad took a deep breath, and then smiled warmly at Tilly. "Enough reminiscing—what were you coming to ask me about?"

Tilly showed him the book she still had tucked under her arm.

"Ah, *Alice in Wonderland*! Perfect research for the party. Can you believe we've never had an Alice theme before in all our years of autumn parties?"

"It's one of Mum's," Tilly explained, passing it to Grandad, who opened the cover automatically and saw the photo that Tilly had shown him yesterday. He stilled for a fraction of a moment before placing his palm on the photo, like it was on the cheek of a child.

"It's a lovely connection to have, isn't it?" Grandad said,

holding the photo up to his glasses. "Having the same book she's reading in the photo. She loved *Alice in Wonderland* too," he said, closing the book and pointing at the cover.

"Do you know why she liked them so much?" Tilly said, remembering her decision to try to find out more about her mother's tastes in books.

"Well, as I said before, she always felt a very personal connection to *A Little Princess*," Grandad said carefully. "And why do any of us love *Alice's Adventures in Wonderland*? Magic, mischief, nonsense, all the good stuff."

"I wish I could talk to her about it," Tilly said.

"Me too, sweetheart," Grandad said. "Me too." He looked into her eyes quite seriously for a moment before an extravagant stomach rumble invaded the silence. "Well then, I suppose I'd best check on lunch. It'll be ready soon. Pop down before too long." He gave her a kiss on the top of her head and set off toward the kitchen.

Tilly found the nearest chair, sat down, and began reading the familiar first few sentences. Soon she was as lost in Wonderland as Alice, reassured by the scenes and characters she knew so well, and soothed by knowing that her mother had made the same journey years before.

6

Trouble Always Starts When You Are Out of Proportion with Whom You Are Talking To

After a lunch of creamy leek and potato soup with chunks of homemade bread and salty butter, Tilly headed out to find Jack, ready to beg or steal something sweet. But before she made it to Jack's café at the back of the ground floor she was struck on the forehead by a jelly bean.

Turning in the direction it had come from, she saw a girl in a full-skirted blue dress sitting on the stairs, lazily throwing jelly beans toward the nearest bookcase.

"Did I hit you? I'm sorry, I was aiming for the cat. Does it have a name? Do you think it likes sweets?"

Tilly stared at her, and the girl widened her eyes in impatience.

"The cat? What's it called? My cat is called Dinah."

"She's called Al—" The girl looked directly at her, and Tilly felt that little itch in her brain. "Alice? She's called Alice?"

"You don't seem very sure about it," the girl said, peering

at Tilly. "But never mind that, because my name is Alice too. How curious."

"Alice," Tilly repeated.

"Yes . . . Al-ice . . ." she said again slowly. "And . . . what . . . is . . . your . . . na—"

"Matilda," Tilly interrupted.

"Whatever your name is, there is always time for good manners; it's very rude to interrupt."

"I'm sorry," Tilly said. "It's nice to meet you, Alice. Um, would you like a cup of tea maybe?"

"Nice to meet you, Matilda," Alice replied, and bobbed a neat curtsy. Tilly tried to copy, but just ended up doing a small, awkward bow. "And thank you, but no thank you. I don't tend to eat or drink in new places until I've thoroughly got my bearings." Alice looked Tilly up and down. "We both seem to be around the same size, though, which is a good sign. Trouble always starts when you are out of proportion with whom you are talking to."

"Are you looking for a book?" Tilly asked.

"Not especially, although I'm never averse to finding a book along my way; they can come in handy sometimes, except you never know what's inside until it's too late, in my experience."

She sighed extravagantly. "Do you know, someone once told me that explanations take such a dreadfully long time that one should focus on adventures, and I've rather come around to their way of thinking. So, if you'll excuse me . . ." And with that Alice skipped toward the back of the bookshop, passing a round little man with a very neat mustache who was coming the other way. The little man gave no indication of having seen her, but gave a neat bow in Tilly's direction.

"*Excusez-moi, mademoiselle.*"

Tilly's head spun, but as she turned round to watch the man leaving she found herself face-to-face with the red-headed girl from that morning. They stared at each other.

"You," the girl said, sounding surprised.

"You!" Tilly said. "You're back! You seem so familiar to me from somewhere; what school do you go to?"

The girl tilted her head to one side and stared hard at Tilly. "I go to school in Avonlea," she said. "Near my home at Green Gables."

"And your name is Anne . . ." Tilly said slowly.

"With an 'e,'" Anne reminded her.

"Anne, with an 'e,' from Green Gables. Anne of Green Gables?"

The girl nodded, still openly staring at Tilly. "But who are you?"

"I'm Tilly! With a 'y.' From here!"

"But you remember me. And, now I am here, I remember you," Anne said in wonder.

"As I said, we literally met this morning," Tilly repeated. "But how can you be Anne of Green Gables? She's not a real person."

"Well, I'm absolutely really here," she said, reaching out and touching Tilly gently on the arm.

"Is this a joke?" Tilly said, looking behind her as if she would see hidden cameras somewhere, or wondering if it was part of some elaborate set-up by Grandad to entertain her during the holidays. "You're from a story?"

"Why, yes," Anne replied happily, not seeming at all perturbed by this fact, and settling herself on the stairs.

"You're real. But you're not real. You're from a book. But you're here," Tilly said, feeling like her brain wasn't quite keeping up with what was happening in front of her.

"Well, why on earth does being from a book mean I'm not real?" asked Anne. "I'm as real as you or this shop, or Julius Caesar or the Lady of Shalott. You can touch my hair, if you'd like, and you will see it is ever so real—to my eternal frustration." Tilly had to admit that Anne's physical presence was undeniable.

"Right," Tilly said, sitting down next to Anne, determined to try to wrap some logic round what seemed to be happening. "Well, what were you doing in Green Gables before you came here? How did you get out?"

"I was sitting in the orchard, imagining all the places I might visit when I am older. And then I was here!"

"But how?" Tilly was almost bursting with frustration.

"I don't know, I just was. I think it is rather marvelous. If you like, I can invent a thrilling story about how I got here with magic spells and a glittering portal. Maybe some kind of benevolent but cursed princess living in a tower who writes poetry and is only allowed a single glass of water each day—"

Tilly interrupted her before she got even more carried away. "But how will you get back? Won't there be gaps in your book spoiling your story somehow, you being here?"

"I'll just go back after I am here. And I don't think it can spoil my story; I rather think only I can spoil my own story."

Tilly sighed and put her head on her knees, and then thought of something.

"Did you see the other girl who was here?" she asked. "Alice?" But when she raised her head Anne was no longer there.

7

Imaginary Friends

An hour or so later, with a slight smell of burned sugar in the air, Jack sent Tilly round to Crumbs with some pop cakes. It had taken him a few batches, but he had finally perfected them so that when you bit into one you got a mouthful of lovely sticky honey. As Tilly stepped onto the street the fresh air and streams of people clutching takeaway coffee cups and mobile phones were reassuringly solid and familiar. Pushing open the door to Crumbs, she saw that Oskar was in his usual spot, this time doodling on a notepad.

"What's that I spy?" Mary said. "Is it an offering from Jack?"

"Yes!" Tilly replied, holding the cake box up. "Pop cakes fresh from the oven! They're best now while the honey is still a bit warm." She opened the box and Mary took one.

"Jack sent enough for Oskar too," Tilly said loudly, and he looked up hopefully.

"Let me bring you two some drinks to have with them," Mary said, pulling another chair up to the table Oskar was sitting at and nudging Tilly into it.

"What are you drawing?" Tilly asked him as she took her coat off. Oskar spread his arms over the paper, like he was trying to stop someone copying a test at school.

"Nothing much, only scribbling. Just something to do," he said.

"Oh, okay," Tilly said, embarrassed at having made him uncomfortable. She messed with the ends of her hair as he painstakingly smoothed a bent corner of paper.

"So, uh, what's your favorite kind of cake?" Oskar asked awkwardly after a pause.

"Carrot cake, I think," Tilly said, surprised at the line of questioning. "What's yours?"

"Red velvet."

"I like that too," Tilly replied, unsure how the conversation had dried up so much since that morning.

"I like carrot cake too."

The silence seemed to solidify around them.

"Anyway, I'm not really very hungry," Tilly said, standing up and banging her knee against the table as her coat sleeve got twisted round the back of her chair. "I was just bringing the cakes over for your mum. See you in school."

"Don't go," Oskar said abruptly, watching Tilly untangle herself. She stopped wrestling with her coat. "I mean, I just wanted to ask which book you decided to read for English homework," Oskar said, picking at his fingernails.

"I think I'm going to read one of my mum's old favorites," Tilly said. "You know I found that box of her books the other day? Well, I thought I might choose one of those that I haven't read yet. Maybe *Treasure Island*?"

"I love that one," Oskar said.

"You've read it?"

"Well, I've listened to the audiobook, if that counts."

"It definitely counts," Tilly said.

They both fell silent as Mary brought them two glasses of orange juice and two pop cakes on patterned plates.

"Everything okay?" she said.

"Yes, fine, thank you," Tilly replied automatically. Then, after a moment, she asked, "Mary, who's your favorite character from a book?"

"What a tricky question." Mary paused in thought as Tilly and Oskar ate their pop cakes. "I think it would have to be Elizabeth Bennet from *Pride and Prejudice*. Have either of you read it?"

Oskar hadn't, but Tilly nodded her head, although she hadn't actually read it; she'd only seen the TV version that her grandma watched every Christmas.

"Do you ever think about what you would say to her, if she was real?" Tilly asked.

"I can't say that I ever have before, Tilly, but it's an

interesting question, isn't it? I suppose I would ask her what it was like in her family, and what Mr. Darcy was really like. I must admit, Tilly, that part of the reason I love her is how much she reminds me of your mum."

"What?" Tilly blurted, remembering the conversation with her grandma earlier.

"Yes, I always thought that Bea had a similar sense of humor to Lizzy's, and your mum was a very sharp observer of people, Tilly—honestly, she used to make me giggle describing some of the customers who came into Pages & Co. Goodness, it would be fun, wouldn't it, to be able to talk to Lizzy Bennet? Although I wonder if she would be like I imagine her, if I actually met her."

"I bet she wouldn't," Oskar said. "I think if you met your favorite character they'd just be disappointing. It would be like meeting a famous person. They wouldn't be as nice as you thought and they probably wouldn't want to talk to you anyway."

"Well, I think it's a lovely idea. If only it were real, eh, Tilly?" Mary laughed and went back to the counter. Tilly looked at Oskar appraisingly.

"Oskar," she whispered, "what would you do if it *was* real?"

"If what was real?" Oskar asked, confused.

"If you could really talk to your favorite characters!"

"I dunno. Ask them stuff? It's not, though, is it? That's the whole point."

Tilly kept going. "But maybe it is."

"But really, Tilly, it isn't. Why are we going round in circles like this?" He sounded bemused.

Tilly took a deep breath. "I'm seeing characters from my favorite books," she announced.

Oskar slowly looked up at her, as though he wasn't sure whether she was having him on. "Tilly—"

"No, don't look like that," Tilly interrupted. "I swear, I was reading my mum's old copy of *Anne of Green Gables* when a girl called Anne with red hair turned up in the bookshop. And then I read *Alice in Wonderland* and a girl called Alice wearing a big blue dress appeared! Oh! *And* I think my grandad might have been talking to Sherlock Holmes as well, and then my grandma was talking to someone she said reminded her of my mum like—"

"Your grandparents think they're seeing book characters too?" Oskar said nervously.

"Oh no. Well, I don't know, I haven't asked them. I need to do some more investigating first."

"Was it your mum's copy of *Alice in Wonderland* as well?" Oskar asked after a pause.

"Yes, from the box of her old books," Tilly explained impatiently.

"And my mum gave you that photo of her yesterday, didn't she?" he went on.

"Yes. And . . . ?"

"Well, don't take this the wrong way," Oskar said quietly, "but do you think maybe it's just been a bit of a weird time with all this stuff about your mum coming up, with the books and the photo, and, um, maybe the characters aren't actually in the shop, you're just imagining them a bit harder than usual. I mean, I definitely had an imaginary friend when I was little—he was called Xavier and he was from Newcastle and he was a redhead—but anyway you don't need to be embarrassed with me. I don't know what I'd do if I didn't have *my* mum around."

Tilly's face flushed hot. "You don't believe me?"

"It's not that I don't believe you, it's just . . ."

"I should have known you wouldn't understand," she said, standing up.

"Why?"

"Because no one ever does."

"Sorry," Oskar said, sounding as embarrassed as she felt, "it's just . . . You know that you're not really talking to fictional characters, don't you?"

Tilly grabbed what was left of her pop cake and walked out without saying goodbye.

8

A Bit of Nonsense Never Hurt Anyone

Tilly didn't pick up her mum's copy of *Alice in Wonderland* again. Instead she chose a brand-new book that she'd never read before and that her mum had definitely never read. She took it over to her favorite sofa only to find it already occupied. At one end was Anne, picking at the ends of her hair. At the other was Alice, looking around impatiently. Tilly waved, a little startled to see them together.

"Oh! How curious," Alice said. "You're just the same as before."

They both stared at Tilly.

"Why wouldn't I be the same? I don't know why you're so surprised. I should be more surprised that you two know each other," Tilly said, and Anne and Alice exchanged another look as if seeing each other properly for the first time.

"Have we met?" Alice said, peering into Anne's face.

"How can you not know if you know each other?" Tilly said. "That doesn't make any kind of sense."

"A bit of nonsense never hurt anyone, did it, carrot-top?" Alice said cheerfully, yanking one of Anne's plaits.

"How dare you!" Anne said. "It's not carrot-colored at all! It is auburn!"

"I only meant it affectionately," Alice insisted. "Your hair is lovely and carroty. One of my very great friends has hair that is a similar color, only most of the time he hides it under a hat. I don't know why you are so touchy about people pointing out what is, after all, a fact that cannot really be denied."

"But it is ever so thoughtless to point out other people's faults," Anne said. "I would hardly come up to you and inform you that you are quite rude and, if we're being brutally honest, that I think you've shrunk since you've been here."

"Well, I am not in charge of that," Alice said crossly. "I cannot help any of it."

"And I am not in charge of the color of my hair," Anne retorted.

"I don't think you would be Anne at all if you didn't have red hair," Tilly offered.

"But when it comes down to it I am not so attached to being Anne," Anne replied. "If, when I was born, I had had beautiful hair as dark as a raven, or blonde hair"—she glanced resentfully at Alice—"then maybe my parents would have been moved to call me something altogether more elegant. Like Ermintrude. Or Cordelia."

"I do not agree at all," Alice said. "Sometimes I feel that my Alice-ness is the only thing I ever know to be true, even when everything around me is acting very strangely indeed. What do you think, Tilly?" And both girls turned to look at her, waiting for an answer.

"Oh, I don't really know. I'm not entirely sure what Tilly-ness is, to be honest, or if I have any of it, or if I'd still have it if I were called something different."

"But Matilda Pages is such a wonderful name to have," Anne said. "It would be a waste if you didn't think about it just a little. It is a name made for adventuring. It's a name to be shouted at the head of an army or whispered in magical forests, don't you think? A name for brave deeds!"

"Be brave, be curious, be kind . . ." Tilly said quietly.

"Why, exactly!" Anne said. "I knew you understood, really."

"I just need an adventure to find me," Tilly said.

"Why, you can't wait for adventure to find you, Matilda," Anne said. "You must go and find adventure, and shake it firmly by the hand as you set out toward the horizon together."

"I agree," Alice said. "That is the first sensible thing you've said. And not to mention you have a whole bookshop with your name to it, Matilda—does it belong to your parents?"

"My parents died when I was a baby," Tilly said, using the

same words she always did when someone asked about them. "It belongs to my grandparents."

"Why, I am an orphan too," Anne said solemnly. Tilly felt a skinny hand take hers and looked down to see Anne's fingers intertwined with her own. "It is not something Alice will understand. It is a difficult thing to bear even if you are surrounded by people who are endlessly kind and good to you. But it is not all woe. I used to think that kindred spirits were hard to find, but look: you have found two just this afternoon."

And, for just that moment, it seemed to be wholly unimportant whether Anne and Alice were real or not.

9

Read Outside Your Comfort Zone

Later that afternoon, long after Alice and Anne had returned to their own stories, Tilly laid out all her mum's books on the floor in her bedroom like jigsaw pieces from different puzzles. She was determined to try to work out at least a little bit of what Tilly-ness meant. Oskar's words about missing her mum circled round her head, and she was determined to find some proof that there was more to what was going on than imaginary friends. Whatever it was, Anne's hand in hers had been resolutely real.

Tilly studied the books laid out in front of her. They were by different authors, from different publishers, and they were different ages and colors. There were adventures and romances, stories about pirates and princesses, and everything in between.

"If this is really happening," Tilly murmured, "then there must be rules. There are always rules for this sort of thing."

She looked for another book she had already read, and was

drawn back again to *A Little Princess*. You could tell it was a favorite: the cover was coming away from the spine and there were several rips in the pages. Wondering if she needed to be in the bookshop for whatever was happening to kick in, she headed downstairs to her reading corner and settled herself there.

"Right, here goes," Tilly said to herself, and opened the book at the first page. She read the first chapter, being sure to pay particular attention to all the details about the main character, Sara, in case that helped. Then she put the book down and waited, but there was no sign of Sara in Pages & Co.

Okay, maybe I need to read more, Tilly thought, and she began to delve further into the book. But the best part of an hour and several circuits of the bookshop later there was still no one matching the description of Sara, or any of the other characters.

Tilly tried books she hadn't read, books that were hers, books that were fresh off the shelves, but there was no one even slightly fictional to be found. She felt a strange mix of disappointment and relief that there didn't seem to be anything more magical than her imagination at play. Maybe Oskar had been right after all.

Finally giving up, Tilly went to find Jack and flung herself dramatically into one of the café chairs, her head still spinning.

"All right, Tils?" Jack called from behind the counter. "That was quite an entrance. I keep telling you that if you stay cooped up in the shop all the time, it'll start getting to you."

Tilly blew her bangs out of her eyes in response.

"Hey, come here. I need some help."

Tilly stood and shuffled her way over to see what Jack was concocting.

"Right, so these are going to be bear pawprint brownies," he said, gesturing at a tray of gooey-looking chocolate brownies cut into squares. "They're an ode to *We're Going on a Bear Hunt*."

He held up a square of baking paper with the shape of a pawprint cut out of the middle and a tiny sieve. "So, I'll hold this template on each brownie and you're going to shake some icing sugar through the sieve, and then, hopefully, we'll peel it off and each one will have a sugar pawprint right in the middle. Got it?"

"I think so," Tilly said, taking the mini sieve and box of icing sugar Jack was holding.

Jack carefully placed the template on the first brownie and nodded to Tilly, who tried to shake some icing sugar into the sieve, but far too much came out and ballooned up, making the air taste sweet around them.

Jack grinned. "Never mind, that's the test one. We can eat it later to check the brownies. Have another go, and maybe shake the box a little slower this time . . ."

Tilly gingerly shook the box, managing to get a light sprinkling of sugar through the sieve and onto a brownie. Jack peeled back the baking paper pattern and gave Tilly a triumphant high five, causing another icing-sugar cloud.

"Who's your favorite book character, Jack?" Tilly asked him as they worked.

"Tough question, Tils. And what do you mean by favorite? The character I like the most, or the character I think is the best written?"

"The character you'd most like to be able to have a real-life conversation with," Tilly replied.

"Oh well, that's a slightly different question," Jack said. "The character I'd most like to talk to . . ." He paused in thought. "I think I would be very tempted to go with Long John Silver, the pirate from *Treasure Island*—have you read that one?"

Tilly shook her head. "I've seen the Muppet film version, though," she offered.

Jack laughed. "Well, I think Robert Louis Stevenson's original version is even better. Think of the stories Silver could tell of pirates and buried treasure. Imagine the debates you could have with him."

"He's a baddie, though, right?" Tilly asked.

"Well, yes, I suppose, technically, but the baddies are more interesting sometimes, don't you think? Or the heroes who aren't always very heroic. People who do the right thing for the wrong reasons or the wrong thing for the right reasons. People like Long John Silver. You should read the original."

"I was a bit put off by the idea of all the boats—I didn't like *Swallows and Amazons*," Tilly said.

"It's not at all like *Swallows and Amazons*. I reckon you'd enjoy it more than you think. I'm sure your grandad has a fancy way of saying you should read outside your comfort zone, and I agree with him."

It was almost closing time and they were still busy decorating brownies when a sharp cough alerted them to the fact that someone else was there.

"I'm so sorry," Jack said, looking up and smiling. "Just decorating brownies . . . bear prints—you see? What can I get you?"

The man standing in front of Jack did not smile back. He was tall and slender, and was wearing a pinstripe suit with a gray bowler hat. His gray tie was held in place with a finely wrought silver tiepin in the shape of an ornate, old-fashioned key. In one hand he held a slim black notebook, and in the other a cane.

"I am looking for Archibald Pages. This is his shop, is it not?" the man said abruptly.

Jack, who was used to dealing with the occasional rude customer, smiled again. "If he's not at the front till, then he's probably at his desk. Is he expecting you?"

"No," the man replied shortly.

"Tilly, why don't you see if you can find your grandad and

ask him if he's free?" Jack said, and the man looked properly at Tilly for the first time.

"You're Archibald's granddaughter?" he said, sounding surprised and staring at her intently.

Tilly nodded.

"How interesting," he said.

"On second thoughts, let me find Archie for you, Mr. . . . ?" Jack paused, waiting for the man to supply his name.

"Chalk. Enoch Chalk. And I can find my own way, thank you. I've been here before." He nodded curtly and set off toward the stairs.

Tilly gave an involuntary shiver as he left. "Goodness, I wonder what he wants with Grandad."

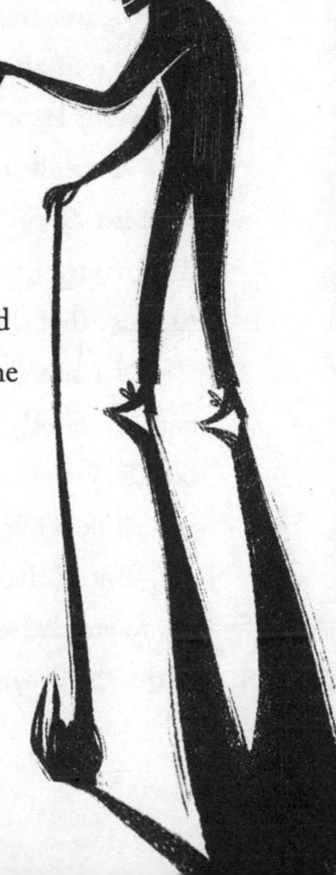

"Oh, probably something boring to do with tax or suchlike. He looked like an accountant, don't you think? Let's get on with the rest of these brownies."

"I think I might go and see if Grandad wants a cup of tea," Tilly said. "I feel like he might need one."

"Good idea, Tils. I'll get a pot brewing."

Tilly didn't exactly mean to sneak up on them, but she did find herself walking particularly

carefully and quietly, and staying out of sight of Grandad's desk. Mr. Chalk had made her feel rather strange, and she wanted to know what business he had with Grandad. By the time she reached the desk their conversation was already heated.

"There have been disturbances in the Sources, Archibald. Things that few people would notice, but which have not escaped my attention."

"Enoch, I don't know what you're talking about. You come barging in here, talking about disturbances as though it was ten years ago. I am not part of this anymore, and you know it."

Tilly leaned closer to the bookshelf she was hiding behind.

"I know that you *should not* be part of this any more, Archibald, but I also know that you could never resist meddling in things that don't concern you—or turning a blind eye to those that should be dealt with."

"Enoch, have you not caused enough problems for me and my family that I have to endure you cropping up in my bookshop?"

"Speaking of family, Archibald—"

But at that moment Tilly wobbled and, putting her hand out to steady herself, pushed several books out of the other side of the shelf, which rained down by the strange man's feet.

"I, um, I was just checking if you wanted a cup of tea?" she tried to say calmly as both men looked up at her and she bent down to pick up the books and hide her red cheeks.

"No. I am leaving," Chalk said, and with a long stare at Tilly but without another word he picked up his notebook and his cane and walked toward the stairs.

"Who was he?" Tilly asked.

Grandad's face was white. "I used to work with him a long time ago; we weren't the best of friends, as you could probably tell."

"What did he mean about disturbances?"

"Were you listening to our conversation, Tilly?" Grandad said sharply.

"No! I just sort of overheard some of it as I was coming over to, you know, ask you about the cup of tea."

"That conversation was private, and not for you to worry about. Chalk is an old colleague whom I didn't see eye to eye with, but what's in the past is in the past, Tilly, and you shouldn't spend any more time thinking about it. Just a bit unexpected, that's all. Now, let's have that brew you mentioned."

They headed to the café in companionable silence, but as Grandad picked up the cup of tea that Jack had poured, Tilly heard the china rattle as his hand shook, even if he did have what was nearly a smile on his face.

10

Fictional by Definition

"Your grandad has used up all the milk again," Grandma said as she opened the fridge. "Would you mind popping out to get some from the corner shop?"

Tilly sighed theatrically.

"Go on, love. I need some for dinner and you haven't been outside all day. Get some Licorice Allsorts for your grandad—you know how much he loves them—and pick something for yourself too." Tilly resignedly took the five-pound note that Grandma handed her and ventured outside.

Everything that had happened so far that day had left Tilly thirsty for glimpses of magic leaking through into the real world, but the street remained resolutely normal around her. She snuggled deeper into her scarf against the wind, but as she went to pull her gloves out of her coat pocket she dislodged the five-pound note that Grandma had given her and it danced down the pavement in front of her. She set off after it, only to crash into someone standing in the middle of the pavement with a white sneaker pinning the money down, stopping it from blowing away.

"Got it," Oskar said, picking up the note and handing it back to Tilly.

"Thanks," she said, tucking it back in her pocket and hopping from one foot to the other in the cold.

"I'm just going to get some milk." Tilly paused. "Do you want to come?"

"Sure," Oskar said. The memory of their last conversation hung awkwardly between them.

Tilly tried to aim for a safe subject as they walked down the street. "Did you have a good afternoon?"

"It was fine," Oskar said.

"Right then," she said, refusing to be the one to make any more effort.

"Sorry, I'm not trying to be rude, honestly, but nothing really happened after you left is all. Just lots of customers and cake. The usual."

"It must be amazing having your mum own a café," Tilly said, her mood thawing quickly. "Almost as good as a bookshop."

"It's okay," Oskar said. "Mum loves it, but I don't think I'd mind if she decided to do something different. I'm not there much since I'm usually in Paris with Dad over the holidays."

"I remember you said. Do you speak much French?"

"A little bit. Dad used to speak French lots when we were

small, but mine gets kind of rusty quickly and then I feel like I get it wrong a lot when I'm in France. My dyslexia doesn't help—it doesn't stick in my brain very well. My dad still has to work a lot when I visit, so I spend quite a bit of time with my French grandma, my *mamie*. We go to lots of museums and galleries: she used to be an illustrator, and she got me into drawing and art and stuff."

"Do you have any friends there?"

"Not really. It's kind of hard to meet other kids when you're not in school. There's a boy in our building who I think must be around our age, but he never seems very friendly. My dad invited him over last summer but he said he couldn't speak any English, even though I'm sure he can."

Oskar was interrupted by a loud laugh from across the street and they both looked up to see a group of girls from their class on the other side of the road.

"Isn't that Grace?" Oskar said.

"Yeah, I think so," Tilly replied.

"She's your friend, isn't she? Do you want to say hi?"

Tilly shrugged. The girls fell about laughing again and Tilly and Oskar both automatically checked themselves for something stuck in their hair, or toilet paper on their shoes.

"I don't think they're laughing at us?" Oskar said, although it came out like a question.

"I don't think they've even noticed us," Tilly said, but at that moment Grace raised her hand in a sort of shy half-wave before seeming to think better of it and running after the rest of the group. Tilly hoped Grace hadn't seen her start to wave back.

"So, you're not friends with Grace anymore?" Oskar asked. The sound of laughter got quieter as the girls turned the corner.

Tilly paused. "I don't really know," she said. She tried to explain. "It's not like you get a letter of resignation or anything. It's just that it got complicated because of secondary school and the netball team and everything."

"Girls are weird," Oskar said.

"Do you really think that?" Tilly said, disappointed.

"No," he replied quickly. "But I mean you can see that it's a bit silly that you and Grace aren't friends because of netball."

"It's not *because* of netball," Tilly said. "It's because of stuff *like* netball. And it's not silly. You thinking girls are weird is silly."

"You know I don't think that at all. I'm sorry," he said. "I just don't understand why friendships aren't easier. Why is it so hard to just find someone you like talking to? That should be all there is to it."

"The problem is that not enough people are best-friend material," Tilly said authoritatively. "And *that's* all there is to it."

"Well, at least you've got your—"

"If you say 'imaginary friends,' I will never speak to you again," Tilly said, staring at him fiercely.

"But, Tilly, they're from books . . . They're imaginary by nature; they're fictional by definition."

"I mean, they are fictional," Tilly said, "but they're not

imaginary! Anyway, I don't want to talk to you about them; you obviously don't get it. You know what, I have to hurry and get the milk for Grandma so she can make dinner. I'll see you later." Tilly sped past Oskar in a self-conscious blur, leaving him scuffing his heels.

Twenty minutes later she thumped the milk down in front of Grandma, who raised her eyebrows.

"Everything okay?"

"Fine," Tilly said, and stormed off.

"Tilly, clearly everything is not fine. Come back and tell me what's going on," Grandma called after her.

"No! Leave me alone. I'm going to read," Tilly shouted back, and Grandma let her go.

Tilly reached the second floor, stewing in her frustration, and there she found Alice sitting primly on the sofa.

"Ah! I've been waiting for you," Alice said, standing up. "Would you like to come to a tea party?"

11

Try to Make a Little More Space for the Impossible to Happen

Tilly stopped short.

"Alice?"

"Yes," Alice said impatiently. "It's very rude to forget someone so quickly after you've first met them, you know."

"No," Tilly protested, "I haven't forgotten you. I just . . . I'd started to wonder if you were really, well, real."

"Why, it's even ruder to question if someone is real." Alice leaned across and pinched Tilly lightly on the arm.

"Ow!" yelled Tilly. "What did you do that for?"

"To prove I am real, obviously," Alice retorted.

"But it's impossible!" Tilly said in frustation.

"I used to be very similar to you," Alice said, patting Tilly on the arm where she had just pinched her, "but so many out-of-the-way things happened to me that I began to think that very few things are indeed really impossible. I know a woman—who spoke a lot of nonsense most of the time, it has to be said—but

she once told me that she sometimes believed as many as six impossible things a day and all before breakfast! So nowadays I try to make a little more space for the impossible to happen." Alice attempted to give Tilly a moment to take in everything she'd said, but couldn't contain herself. "Anyway, do you want to come to a tea party or not? You said yourself that you want to be more curious."

Tilly looked up and steeled herself. "Why not? How much stranger could things get?"

Alice bounced excitedly next to her and held out her hand.

Tilly shrugged and took hold of it.

All at once Pages & Co. seemed to divide into a grid of tiny tiles that click-clacked over each other like a wooden toy folding down on itself.

In only a few seconds the whole shop had dominoed down and seemed to wind itself in under Tilly and Alice as if pulled to them by a very powerful magnet.

Tilly's stomach dropped, like the moment you go over the top of a roller coaster, and there was a smell of marshmallows toasting on a bonfire. Instead of the familiar bookshop, Tilly and Alice were standing in a colorful forest, with a thatched house tucked into the trees and a long table set out in front of it. At one end of the table sat a large hare in a bow tie, a dormouse who seemed to be asleep, and a man wearing a rather mad-looking hat.

"Oh. You were talking about *this* tea party," Tilly said queasily.

Alice nodded merrily. "Welcome to Wonderland! It's always teatime here. Let me introduce you," she said, skipping over to the table. "And please don't mind them if they are a little rude until they get to know you, and quite likely for a while after that as well."

Tilly followed Alice to the table, not quite believing that she could feel the grass under her feet and touch the wooden chair she was about to sit down on.

"No room! No room!" the hare shouted, and Tilly felt a strange sense of déjà vu. Was this the exact scene from the book she had read so many times?

"Why, there's plenty of room," Alice said sternly. "We've been over this before." She nodded encouragingly at Tilly. "Go on, sit down. It's fine."

Tilly perched on the edge of the huge, squishy cushion covering the chair and smiled nervously at the characters she knew so well who were now staring at her haughtily.

"Would you like some cake?" the Hatter asked, gesturing at the table, which was entirely free of anything to eat and held only teapots and teacups.

"No thank you," Tilly said. "May I have a cup of tea, please?"

"I am ever so sorry, but we are completely out of tea. So sorry, so sorry. Would you like some wine?" the Hatter said, while pouring himself a cup of tea.

"I can't drink wine, I'm eleven," Tilly said, confused.

"I'm ever so sorry," the Hatter replied. "How foolish of me; you are far too old to be drinking wine at teatime."

"Too old?"

"Why, yes. One should have long broken the habit of wine drinking if one is already eleven. Your discipline is commendable, and we shall all be most inspired by it. Some tea?" he said.

"Well, yes. I wanted tea to begin with," Tilly said.

"There's no need to be demanding," the Hatter said, filling up a fresh teacup and then drinking it himself. "Do you like riddles?" he asked.

"Not particularly—" Tilly started.

"Wonderful! Do tell us some. We love a riddle to ponder over tea."

"I'm really sorry, but I don't think I know any riddles," Tilly protested.

"Well, make one up," the Hatter said sternly.

At that moment the dormouse woke up.

"You stole my butter knife!" it squawked, before going back to sleep. The hare looked expectantly at Tilly as she racked her brains for any riddles.

"Okay, I've got one. What flies without wings?" she tried.

"Easy!" yelled the hare, thumping his paw onto the table and making all the teacups dance and rattle. "Time! And we don't speak of him around these parts. Next! Do try harder with the next one."

Tilly desperately tried to remember another riddle. "How about . . . What belongs to you, but others use it more than you do?" The hare paused, and stroked his chin.

The dormouse woke again. "Teaspoons," he said. "Everyone is always stealing my teaspoons."

The hare nodded solemnly. "Yes, teaspoons. These teaspoons belong to me, but are used much more by others, and often used not at all properly." He glared at Alice, who was watching the conversation with delight.

"No, the answer isn't teaspoons," Tilly said a little crossly. "The answer is your name. Your name belongs to you, but others use it more than you do."

"You might as well say that your birthday belongs to you," the Hatter chimed in.

"You may as well claim your age belongs to you," the dormouse called.

"My birthday does belong to me! And so does my age. I think. Oh, I'm not at all sure."

"But you share both with an awful lot of other people," said the hare. "My teaspoons belong only to me. And I would like them all back now, if you please," he said, and yanked a teaspoon out of Alice's hand as he spoke.

"What did you mean when you said you don't speak of time around these parts?" Tilly asked, trying to change the subject.

"The Hatter had a bit of a quarrel with Time," Alice explained quietly. "The Hatter was singing in a concert for the Queen of Hearts, and the queen accused him of murdering the time, and since then, why, Time won't help the Hatter out at all. He used to be ever so helpful with getting things straightened out. That's why it's always teatime here; Time has made it stick at six o'clock."

At this the Hatter burst into noisy tears. "It was such a beautiful song as well; shall I sing it for you?" He looked beseechingly at Tilly, who wasn't at all sure if she wanted to hear it until Alice kicked her under the table.

"Please do," Alice said politely.

"Yes, I'm sure it's beautiful," Tilly agreed, trying to kick Alice back, but instead banging her knee hard on the leg of the table.

The Hatter wiped his nose with a very frilly sleeve, pushed back his chair, and stood, and Tilly was surprised to see that he didn't appear much taller when he stood up than he did sitting down. He cleared his throat and began, to a tune that sounded remarkably similar to "Twinkle, Twinkle, Little Star":

"Twinkle, twinkle, little bat!
How I wonder what you're at!
Up above the world you fly,
Like a tea tray in the sky.
Twinkle, twinkle . . ."

And at this point the dormouse and hare both started swaying along and chanting "Twinkle, twinkle, twinkle" to no recognizable tune at all, and the Hatter closed his eyes and started humming to himself as the dormouse fell asleep again.

Alice clapped delightedly. "Bravo! Bravo!"

Tilly clapped too, a little more hesitantly, as the Hatter bowed and sat back down.

"Well now, do you know any songs, girl?" the hare said to Tilly. "Or any stories?" he added hopefully.

"Oh no, I couldn't possibly," Tilly said, shrinking back into her seat.

"Boring!" shouted the hare.

"Do you know I had heard you were rude," Tilly snapped, "but I didn't imagine you would be quite so rude as this."

"Who told you I was rude?" the hare said. "What a terribly ill-mannered thing to say about someone. Was it that grinning Cheshire Cat?"

"Oh no," Tilly said, immediately feeling bad. "Maybe I misheard, I'm sorry."

"Boring!"

At that the dormouse raised his head again. "Enough of all this. And anyway, who is that and does he want any tea?" he said, gesturing with a lazy paw. Everyone turned to see a tall man in a gray bowler hat sitting at the far end of the long table.

Tilly's blood ran cold. It was Mr. Chalk, the man who had visited Grandad in the bookshop.

"Why are you here?" she asked, but everyone spoke at once and her question was drowned out by the noise.

"How long have you been sitting there?" shouted Alice.

"Would you like some tea?" said the dormouse.

"You need a haircut," said the Hatter.

"Are you using one of my teaspoons?" the hare said suspiciously.

Tilly looked at Alice, panicked. "Alice, Alice," she whispered, trying to get her attention without the others noticing. "Alice! That man was in the bookshop the other day, talking to Grandad! What's he doing here?" But when she looked back up to where Chalk had been sitting he was gone.

"Oh, he must be a friend of the Cheshire Cat," Alice said. "Although I've never seen him here before."

"I think I want to go home," Tilly said to Alice.

"Really? But you've only just arrived," said Alice.

"Yes, really. I really do want to go home."

"Already?"

"Yes, already!"

"If you insist," Alice said, and grasped her hand under the table.

This time everything seemed to happen in reverse: the tiles of Pages & Co. folded out from underneath them, stacking upward as the walls of reality righted themselves around them, blocking out the tea party until Tilly was sitting in the bookshop again.

She slumped back against the sofa. "Alice, what was that?" she said breathlessly. But when she turned to her side Alice was no longer there.

Tilly was not sure how long she had been sitting on the sofa, breathing heavily, when her grandma's voice interrupted her.

"Tilly, could you come and help with dinner?" she shouted up the stairs.

"Coming," Tilly called, shaking her head as if trying to dislodge the memory of what had just happened.

"Are you okay, sweetheart?" Grandma asked as they topped and tailed green beans side by side. "You've been out of sorts today. Is whatever bothered you when you went to the shops still playing on your mind?"

"I just had a weird afternoon," Tilly said tentatively. "I bumped into Oskar and we kind of disagreed about something, and then when I got back here I met some, well, unusual people."

"In the bookshop?" Grandma said. "You know you don't have to talk to any customers if you don't want to, and you can come and get one of us or Jack at any point."

"It wasn't like that," Tilly said. "I kind of knew them already."

Grandma frowned. "Kind of? Were they from school? You're talking in circles, Tils."

"It's been that sort of day," Tilly said.

"Okay, sweetheart, well, I'm here if you want to talk about it more. Speaking of friends from school, is there anyone you want to invite to the party on Wednesday? Oskar maybe?"

"Maybe," Tilly said, still smarting from her last conversation with him. "Grandma, do you ever feel as if you read books, like, more than other people?"

"Well, yes, of course. I read books for my job, so I definitely read more books than lots of people, although several of our regulars certainly like to tell me about everything I haven't read," she said, carrying on trimming the beans.

"No, I don't mean more books; I mean, do you read more intensely, I guess? Like, sometimes when you're reading do you feel like you're really there or something?"

Grandma turned and looked intently at Tilly just as the phone rang, startling them both. Grandma's knife slipped, catching the tip of her finger.

"Oh shoot," she said, grabbing a nearby tea towel and pressing it on to her finger, which was undramatically but consistently leaking blood.

"Tilly, I very much want to talk more about this, but right now I need you to go quickly and get me the first-aid box from the bathroom."

Tilly nodded and went to get the box as the phone rang off. By the time Grandma's finger had been thoroughly cleaned and bandaged their conversation seemed to have been forgotten.

12

An Active Imagination

The next morning brought a sheepish-looking Oskar to Pages & Co. carrying the book Tilly had helped him to pick out.

"Hey," he opened with.

"Hi," Tilly said shortly.

"Can I come and hang out here for a bit?"

"I guess."

"It's really busy at Crumbs because of half-term and Mum says I can't take up table space." Tilly nodded and went back to her book. Oskar shuffled his feet awkwardly. "Um, where should I sit?" Tilly was in an armchair and there was nowhere else free apart from the floor. She made a big performance of standing up and gathering together her bits and pieces.

"We can go to the third floor, I guess. It's always quiet there, plus no kids come up so the beanbags stay nice and clean. I brought them up from the children's floor to protect them."

They went upstairs and settled themselves into the colorful beanbags nestled behind the philosophy shelves.

"I'm sorry about yesterday," Oskar blurted out. "I didn't mean to sound like I was laughing at you, or that I thought you were silly."

"I know the characters I'm seeing are fictional," Tilly conceded, glad that he'd raised the subject again. "But that doesn't mean they're not real. I don't know what's happening but I promise I'm not making it up."

"I know," Oskar said. "I'm not sure I know what's going on either, but I believe you. Who did you say you'd seen? Your favorite characters, right?"

"Yes," Tilly said, relief washing over her. "I saw Alice from Wonderland and Anne Shirley from *Anne of Green Gables*. Anne was just like I'd hoped, although Alice is kind of blunt."

"I sort of wish *I* was seeing fictional characters," Oskar said, scratching his forehead. "There are plenty of everyday people I like fine, but I'm not sure I'd count on them as friends, if it came down to it."

"Apart from me," Tilly said quietly after a beat.

"Apart from you," Oskar agreed with a smile that reached all the way to his eyes.

They were interrupted by the sound of Grandma and Grandad coming upstairs, and sitting down on the other side of the bookcase, where Oskar and Tilly were hidden from view.

"We need to talk about Tilly," they heard Grandma say.

Oskar and Tilly exchanged a look. Oskar gestured to see if they should move, but Tilly shook her head fiercely and put her finger to her lips. Oskar looked uncomfortable, but stayed put.

"You know what I'm talking about, Archie," Grandma said when Grandad didn't reply. "Yesterday, she asked me if I sometimes felt like I was really inside a book when I read. Do you think it's happened?"

"She's always had an active imagination, Elsie. Could it just be that?" Grandad said.

"You know it's more than that, Archie—and she found those books of Bea's. That could have been the trigger—you know there's often one along those lines . . . She hasn't asked about him, has she?"

"No, not yet."

"But, Archie, far more concerning at the moment is the fact that she seems to be able to see Holmes and Lizzy. You know that shouldn't be possible."

"I know, I know," Grandad said quietly. "There's something else. I should have told you straightaway, but I hoped it was nothing. It's about Chalk." Oskar and Tilly heard Grandma take a sharp breath. "He was here, Elsie; he came to the shop. He was asking about disturbances at the Library, and he met Tilly."

"Tilly? Does he know who she is? And what disturbances? What did you say?" Grandma asked.

"I told him I had no clue what he was talking about, of course. And yes, he knew she was my granddaughter. I had hoped he would never have found out about Tilly," he said, sighing.

"What do we do?" Grandma asked quietly.

"I don't know. Wait and see what happens, I suppose. Keep a close eye on Tilly. What else can we do?"

"Is it worth speaking to Amelia, do you think?"

"Not yet," Grandad said. "It could all still blow over."

"I hope you're right, Archie," Grandma said, and they heard her stand up. At that Oskar and Tilly scrunched down into their beanbags, trying not to be seen, and they heard Grandad head upstairs to his desk and Grandma going back downstairs to the till.

Oskar looked at Tilly. She felt a little sick.

"Do you know what they're talking about, Tilly?" he whispered.

She shook her head. "But there's definitely something weird going on."

Oskar shrugged helplessly at her.

"Speaking of which, things sort of escalated yesterday . . ." she went on. "To start with it was characters coming *out* of their books into Pages & Co. and talking to me," Tilly explained.

"To start with . . . ?" Oskar said nervously.

"Yes, because yesterday Alice took me to the Mad Hatter's tea party," Tilly said all in a rush.

"To the Mad Hatter's tea party . . ." Oskar repeated slowly.

"To *actual* Wonderland," Tilly said, in case he didn't understand yet.

"And how, exactly, did you get there?" Oskar asked.

"Well, we were here, and then I held Alice's hand, and everything sort of fell down around us, and behind everything normal was Wonderland," she explained.

The silence that followed was eventually interrupted by a sad sniffle, and Tilly looked up to see Anne leaning against a bookshelf, about to burst into tears.

"I can't believe she did that," Anne said mournfully.

"You can't believe who did what?" Tilly said.

"Who did what?" Oskar repeated in confusion.

"Alice!" Anne said.

"Not you—Anne!" Tilly said at the same time.

"What?" Oskar said.

"Oh—he can't see or hear me," Anne said in an offhand manner as if that was the least pressing thing to deal with.

"Oh goodness," Tilly said.

She turned to Oskar, who still looked utterly bemused. "So . . . Anne is here," she said, not sure how to prove to him what was going on.

"Anne . . . ?"

"Anne of Green Gables. From the book. Like I said!"

"Tilly, there's no one here but us," Oskar said, gesturing around them.

"Anne, why can't he see you? Can you do something about it?" Tilly said desperately. "Can you, like, knock something over or something?"

"I'm not some kind of performing monkey, Matilda," Anne said woefully. "He can't see me because I'm yours. The only way he could see me would be if you both . . . Oh, but I shouldn't." Anne looked over at Oskar thoughtfully. "Actually I don't see why not, considering the circumstances . . ."

"What are you—" Tilly started, but in one swift movement Anne leaned down and took both Oskar and Tilly by the shoulders, and the burned marshmallow smell filled the air as the walls of the shop seemed to topple down around them, leaving them standing in a startlingly beautiful wood with late-afternoon sun dripping through the leaves above them.

Anne breathed in the fresh air in delight.

Oskar fell to his knees and was sick in the bushes.

"First time?" Anne asked kindly, giving him a pat on the back. "It can make your stomach feel a little bit funny. But it's lovely to meet you properly. I'm Anne. With an 'e,'" she said, sticking her hand out.

Oskar shook it feebly, still looking rather worse for wear. "Where are we?"

"We're in Avonlea, of course!" Anne said. "Come on, we're going to be late for school."

"We've traveled magically inside a book and now we're going to school?" Oskar said to Tilly, looking horrified, but they didn't have time to argue as Anne had already set off briskly through the trees and they were left with no choice but to follow her.

13

The Story Is the Thing

Tilly and Oskar followed Anne's bobbing red plaits up a thin, twisting path with tightly packed, silvery trees on either side. Around the feet of the trees were flowers and plants of all different kinds, and Tilly could hear birds above them and the wind whispering. She was not sure she had ever been in such a lovely place before.

"This is the Birch Path," Anne called back to them as they jogged to catch up with her. "Diana named it. Diana is my best friend in the whole world," Anne explained to Oskar. "I know the name is a little unimaginative, but I try very hard to let people with less imagination than me join in too." She pointed up the hill. "If you go farther that way, you get to Mr. Bell's woods, and down in the valley is Avonlea school, where we're headed. And then, if you go even farther that way, you'll see Green Gables."

Oskar was still very quiet, stumbling over his feet as he stared around as they walked.

"Tilly, are we really inside a book? I don't . . . How is that even possible?"

"I don't know any of the answers either," Tilly said. "This is only the second time it's happened to me."

"Excuse me," Oskar said, tapping Anne on the shoulder. "I don't mean to sound rude but are you real? Is this real?"

"Depends on what you mean by real," Anne said. "Does this feel real?" She picked up a twig from the ground and poked Oskar in the side with it.

"Yes! Ow!" he said. "So you know you're a character from a book?"

"Yes, of course, although the story is the thing, not where it's written down. You're thinking about it too hard."

"I hate it when books don't explain how everything works," Tilly muttered. "It's all very well saying that it's magical and wonderful, but what happens if I'm sucked into something like *Animal Farm* and get stuck there?"

"*Animal Farm* sounds lovely!" Anne said.

"You wouldn't say that if you'd read it," Tilly said, feeling slightly mutinous.

"Have either of you ever been to Canada before?" Anne asked as the three of them ambled along.

"Wait, we're in Canada?" Oskar stopped walking abruptly, but Tilly and Anne ignored him.

"No, never," Tilly said. "I've never been abroad at all. Oskar lives in France sometimes, though."

"Sorry, can we go back to us being in Canada?" Oskar said, catching up.

"Well, Avonlea, where we are now, is in Canada, therefore we are all in Canada, you see?" Anne said in a kindly tone as if she was speaking to a small child.

"But how did we get to Canada?"

"Because I live in Canada."

"Right, but how did we get here from London?"

"You came with me!" Anne said, her patience fraying.

"Okay, guys, stop, please," Tilly said. "Can this wait? Oskar, we are in Avonlea, where Anne is from—that's what matters. We are in her life, in her story, like I told you about Alice."

"I still can't believe Alice took you to hers first," Anne said, obviously still smarting. "But I got Oskar!"

"Yay," Oskar said weakly.

"Do you truly live in France sometimes?" Anne asked. "How awfully romantic. That must be a very long journey. Some of the folks around here can speak a bit of French, but I can't at all."

"Yes, I really do. My dad lives there," Oskar explained.

"By himself?" Anne said.

"With my sister. My parents got divorced a while ago."

Anne looked scandalized.

"It's pretty normal where we're from," he said.

"You are very fortunate to have both of your parents," Anne said solemnly, linking arms with Tilly. "For we are both orphans. I haven't met many other orphans since I came to Avonlea," she

said, turning to Tilly. "I rather thought it might mean we were kindred spirits. You see, Diana is my absolute best friend in the whole world, but she has two parents who care for her so much that I sometimes think that she doesn't quite understand the plight of an orphan, even if I have found somewhere I might belong at Green Gables. Do you remember them at all, your parents?"

"No," said Tilly shortly. "My dad died before I was born and we don't know what happened to my mum. She disappeared when I was still a baby."

"How simply awful," Anne said. "It is such a cross to bear not truly knowing one's own mother and father. I like to imagine details about mine sometimes to try to make up a little of the loss. The facts of the matter are that my parents were called Walter and Bertha, and they were schoolteachers who died of a fever when I was only three months old. But I imagine so much more about them. I imagine that my father used to love reading poetry aloud to my mother by a roaring fire, and that my mother made excellent currant cake, and that for a treat at Christmastime they would go for a sleigh ride across the snow. Do you ever imagine things about your own parents?"

"Well, the other day . . ." Tilly stopped, feeling self-conscious, but Anne squeezed her arm and nodded encouragingly. "The other day I was sitting in my room and I imagined that my mum was downstairs in the kitchen, helping make dinner with my grandma. Is that silly?"

"Why, not at all!" Anne said. "It is a lovely thing to imagine. And what about your father?"

"I don't imagine things about him so much," Tilly said. "My grandparents didn't know him very well so they don't have any of the little details about him that they have about my mum. My parents weren't married, you see; they hadn't known each other very long."

Anne let out a gasp before clapping her hand over her mouth as if she could put it back in. Her cheeks reddened.

"Honestly, all this is a lot more common where we're from; lots of people's parents aren't married. It's just the way things are sometimes. There are all kinds of different-shaped families." Tilly watched Anne trying to process all of this. "I do have this of my mum's," she said, pulling out the delicate bee necklace and showing it to Anne. "Her name was Bea, short for Beatrice. She had a matching necklace to this one—my father gave it to her and she got one for me."

"How awfully romantic," Anne said wistfully.

At that moment they stepped out of the woods onto a wide red-sand road lined with spruce trees, and Anne immediately jolted out of her reverie and started fizzing with excitement as she gestured to the top of the hill, where Tilly could see Avonlea school, a whitewashed wooden building with big windows.

"Now," said Anne, "let me just set you straight about a few things. You need to watch out for the Pye girls, who are not to be trusted, and Prissy Andrews is ever so elegant but not quite so smart, although it isn't very generous of me to say so, and Marilla scolds me if I do. Prissy is the one with the beautiful curly brown hair. And, of course, there is Diana, who you will adore as much as I do. But I am fond of Ruby and Sophia and Jane too—and oh, of course, there's another girl called Tillie, and she let me wear her ring all afternoon the other week because I admired it so much. And there's Mr. Phillips, our teacher. And look! Here comes Diana!" Her face lit up as a girl with glossy black hair raced down the hill toward them.

"Diana, these are my friends Tilly and Oskar, who are visiting and are going to come to school with us!"

Diana didn't even pause to question this but launched herself into a hug with Tilly before giving Oskar a polite little curtsy.

"How wonderful! And what a good day to visit as you'll be able to meet Gilbert too!" she added conspiratorially. "He is such a tease, but he's awfully handsome. He's nearly fourteen, you know. He's always top of the class."

"Well, I would hope so if he's three years older than you," Oskar said.

"Oh, but he's only in our class because his father was awfully sick and went to recuperate in Alberta and Gilbert went with him. You mustn't say anything like that to him because it was terribly noble of Gilbert to go with his father and tend to him, and he didn't have the opportunity to go to school much in Alberta, you see," Diana said sternly as they walked into the schoolroom.

The classroom was remarkably familiar, despite the old-fashioned clothes and desks; children were hugging and shouting and arguing and laughing, hanging up coats and hats, but pulling out slates and chalk instead of paper and pens. The children acted in much the same way as the children in Tilly and Oskar's school too; Tilly could see one group of girls obviously laughing at another girl, and a boy tipping what looked suspiciously like ink into another boy's satchel.

Tilly felt a familiar discomfort settle on her that seemed inextricably linked to classrooms. She tried to take it all in and reassure herself that this was a different classroom, in a different time, full of different—not to mention fictional—people.

Anne maneuvered Tilly toward a double desk with a space next to a girl with a long blonde plait, and pointed Oskar toward a free desk near the back of the classroom.

Oskar stumbled toward it and stared wide-eyed at the children piling in, sitting down gingerly as if he expected to go right through a chair that couldn't possibly really be there.

As everyone started to settle Tilly's eye was caught by a movement behind her, and she saw a tanned arm slowly reach for the blonde girl's plait. Before she knew it, the end of the plait had been pinned to the back of the seat with a tack.

Tilly turned to see a boy with curly hair and brown eyes

put a finger to his lips as Mr. Phillips asked for volunteers to help hand out the slates. Before Tilly could do anything, the girl had stood up and was yanked backward as her hair caught and she let out a piercing shriek, causing everyone to turn and stare at their desk. The girl sat back down and began to cry. Tilly quickly pulled the pin out of the desk and tentatively rubbed the girl's arm in what she hoped was a comforting sort of way. She turned to Anne for guidance, but Anne was glaring fiercely at the boy in utter disgust. He merely winked at her, causing Anne's cheeks to blush raspberry.

"Gilbert," Tilly said under her breath.

14

An Excellent Plot Twist

Tilly found it hard not to stare at Anne as, despite the hard wooden seats and smell of chalk in the air, there was still a dreamy quality to the whole affair. Anne was just like Tilly had always imagined her: she spent the morning mostly staring out of the classroom window, lost in her own daydreams. Tilly saw Gilbert trying to get Anne's attention several times, making silly faces and scratching his chalk so it made horrible screeches that annoyed everyone apart from his intended target. After failing to get her to notice him, Gilbert leaned across and pulled one of Anne's red plaits hard.

"Carrots! Carrots!" Gilbert whispered, quiet enough to avoid the attention of the teacher but loud enough for most of the students to hear him.

Anne leaped up, fighting back angry tears, and grabbed the slate from her desk.

"You mean, hateful boy!" she shouted. "How dare you!"

And with that she cracked it over Gilbert's head. Tilly heard Oskar yelp at the back of the room.

The classroom erupted in shouts, gasps, and more tears from Tilly's desk-mate, and the tumult finally distracted Mr. Phillips from the sums he was writing on the board.

"Anne Shirley, what is the meaning of this?" he shouted.

Anne was still standing, staring at Gilbert, with one half of her cracked slate in each hand.

Gilbert spoke first. "It was my fault, Mr. Phillips. I teased her."

But Mr. Phillips was having none of it. "I am sorry to see a pupil of mine displaying such a temper and vindictive spirit," he said.

"Oh, she hardly has a vindictive spirit! Gilbert *was* teasing her," Tilly said, not able to help herself.

Mr. Phillips turned to look at her, noticing her for the first time.

Tilly felt herself shrink under his gaze. "I just mean . . . Gilbert was being rude and . . . I didn't mean to . . ." she faltered.

"Who, exactly, are you?" he said imperiously. "Are you a new student? Why wasn't I informed that you were to be starting?"

Mr. Phillips's scolding drew Anne's attention from Gilbert finally.

"That is Tilly Pages and she is my friend who is visiting. Sir," Anne added begrudgingly.

"Well, both of you will go and stand at the front and write lines for the entirety of the afternoon. I will not tolerate this sort of behavior in my classroom. And you," he said, looking down his nose at Tilly, "have made a very weak first impression."

Tilly exchanged a horrified look with Oskar. Whatever difficulties their school threw up, neither of them had ever been asked to write lines at the front of the class for a whole afternoon. Mr. Phillips walked in front of them to the blackboard and on one side wrote:

Ann Shirley has a very bad temper. Ann Shirley must learn to control her temper.

And on the other side:

Tillie Pages has a quick tongue. Tillie Pages must learn to control her tongue.

Anne looked across at her mournfully. "I am so sorry for dragging you down into my shame; I just can't believe Gilbert would call me 'carrots,' and in front of everyone. Oh, and Mr. Phillips has spelled your name wrong as well, to add insult to injury."

"You'll have to use my extra 'e's," Tilly whispered.

Oskar, meanwhile, slumped down in his chair and tried to avoid drawing any attention to himself at all.

The endless lines made the afternoon a lot less enjoyable than the morning, and Tilly almost wished for the monotony of her usual classroom. When it was finally over and Tilly, Oskar, Diana, and Anne left the schoolroom they found Gilbert waiting for them, running his hand through his messy curls awkwardly.

"I'm awfully sorry I made fun of your hair, Anne," he said, looking genuinely worried. "Honest I am. Don't be mad for keeps now."

But Anne simply tossed her head and pulled Diana and Tilly along with her, with Oskar awkwardly following.

"Oh, how could you, Anne?" Diana said, scandalized, and tried to turn back to look at Gilbert, before Anne tugged her onward.

"I shall never forgive Gilbert Blythe," said Anne, striding onward. "Never."

After the group had waved Diana off up the hill toward her house, Anne threw herself down onto a grassy verge by the path. "I am thoroughly embarrassed that you had to witness such a display," she said. "I work so hard to maintain my poise in trying situations, but it does not come very naturally to me."

"You shouldn't feel embarrassed at all," Tilly said. "I thought you were wonderful. I wish I was brave enough to stand up for myself like you did. I think everyone else was very much on your side, and look how bad Gilbert felt afterward."

"Don't even say his name to me, Tilly," Anne said, though

her cheeks glowed with pleasure. "I won't utter it from now onward. What do you think, Oskar?"

"Uh, about whether to ever say his name again? I feel like it might get impractical," Oskar offered.

"No, do you think he felt terrible afterward?" Anne asked.

"I guess?"

"Just as I thought," Anne said with a satisfied grin on her face.

Their conversation was interrupted by a tapping sound coming up the path toward them. Tilly felt as though the air had been sucked from her lungs when she saw the man in the gray bowler hat come round the corner.

She elbowed Oskar urgently in the side. "That's Mr. Chalk. The man my grandparents were talking about. Anne, I don't know why he's here," she whispered. "He was in the bookshop, talking to Grandad, and he was at Alice's tea party too."

"He was talking to your grandad?" Oskar said, frowning.

"Yes. He was talking about a library."

"Well, he's heading our way, and he certainly has a very sour-looking face, doesn't he?" Anne said, raising herself onto her elbows.

Chalk neared where the three

of them were now standing and doffed his hat at them, a thin smile on his face that didn't even nearly reach his eyes.

"Matilda," he said coldly. "Out and about again, I see?"

"Who are you?" Tilly said, ignoring his question. "Are you following me?"

"My name is Mr. Chalk," the man said. "I used to work with your grandfather a long while ago. And don't be so self-centered, child. I'm merely out for a wander. Checking the borders, as it were. Just a happy coincidence to run into you, and with a friend as well," he said, nodding toward Oskar.

Tilly didn't trust herself to say anything.

"Does Tilly's grandad know about all of this?" Oskar said, gesturing vaguely around.

Chalk made a noise like a giggle laced with a sneer. It was the worst sound Tilly had ever heard.

"Has your grandfather told you nothing?" Chalk said. "How interesting. An excellent plot twist, you might even say." He looked around as if wanting applause. "I wonder . . . But no, I'll let you get back home then, children. It sounds like you need to have a tête-à-tête with your grandfather. Perhaps we'll run into each other again sooner than we think." And with that he tapped his way up the path.

Tilly shivered, even though the sun was still warm and high above the trees.

"Can you take us home, please, Anne?" she said quietly.

Anne sighed as though their leaving was the saddest possible thing she could imagine, but held out her hands. Tilly and Oskar both took one and the moment they were all linked the woods melted away as the familiar surroundings of Pages & Co. folded out and up around them. Just before the real world had settled and solidified, Anne smiled and let go and melted back into her story, leaving them standing in the bookshop.

"I think we need to talk to your grandad," Oskar said.

They found him sitting at his desk with a cup of coffee and one of Jack's croissants. He smiled absentmindedly as they came over. "Lovely to see you, Oskar. How are you getting on with that book?"

"Grandad," Tilly said, and he looked up as he registered her solemn tone.

"What's happened?" he said urgently.

"Grandad, we need to ask you about something," Tilly said, and he blanched. "We just got back from a book."

"Like, *inside* a book," Oskar said.

"Specifically, *Anne of Green Gables*," Tilly added.

"Together? You were both in *Anne of Green Gables* at the same time? That really is most unusual," Grandad said almost to himself.

"I think we're way past unusual," Oskar said.

"Well, I suppose I knew this day was going to come eventually," Grandad said, taking a deep breath. "I think it's time for you to meet the Librarian."

15

It Just Felt Like the Right Book

"The what?" Tilly said.

"The who?" Oskar said at the same time.

"As you have no doubt worked out," Grandad said briskly, "considering where you've just been, there is a little more to Pages & Co. than most customers ever see. In fact," he said, looking curiously at Oskar, "it's not something most customers ever see, and something that not all readers are able to do. But it's better if the Librarian explains it all to you—that's how we do things."

"We?" asked Oskar, but he was ignored again.

"Are we going right now?" Tilly said in surprise.

"Not right now, no, but we do need to go relatively soon. There are some basics we need to get covered to keep you safe, especially if you're being dragged into books, even if it's just to Avonlea. It's a good job you're not an avid *Lord of the Rings* reader or we'd have to deal with this even more urgently. Let's go and ask Mary if she's happy for Oskar to come with us into town later today."

"I can go and ask her," Oskar said quickly. "I'm sure today will be fine. Where are we going? Do I need a packed lunch? An umbrella?"

"Oskar, this isn't a school trip; this is all more complicated than you could possibly know," Grandad said.

"It's more complicated than the fact that we just traveled inside a book? It's more complicated than the fact that Alice from *Alice in Wonderland* just pops into Pages & Co. for a little chat with Tilly now and again? It's more complicated than some sinister man following Tilly through books?" Oskar said in disbelief.

"It is considerably more complicated than that, yes, Oskar," Grandad replied. "Hang on. What did you say about a sinister man following Tilly? A character in one of the books?"

"No," Tilly explained. "It was that man who came to visit you here the other day—Mr. Chalk."

"And he was in *Anne of Green Gables*?"

"And *Alice in Wonderland*," Tilly added.

"You've been to Wonderland too?" Grandad shook his head. "And he was there at the same time as you and Oskar?"

Tilly nodded.

"But he didn't enter the book at the same time as you two? Are you sure?"

"Absolutely sure."

"Did Chalk say anything to you, Tilly?"

"He was just all weird and creepy and then he left. He said he knew you from work, and he laughed when he realized you hadn't told me about it," Tilly said quietly.

"Okay. Okay. Right, Oskar, you go back to—"

"But—" Oskar protested.

"Hear me out," Grandad said. "You go back to Crumbs and ask your mum if you can come with us into King's Cross this afternoon. Tell her I'm taking you two to the British Library. Tilly and I will come by to pick you up in a bit—text Tilly or pop back in if there's a problem."

Oskar was about to launch into a new list of questions, but at the unsettled look on Tilly's face he swallowed his queries, closed his mouth, and nodded.

Grandad squeezed him firmly on the shoulder. "Thank you, Oskar. We'll see you soon. Now, Tilly, let's find your grandma."

Grandma was behind the till, chatting animatedly to a regular customer.

"You are coming to the party on Wednesday, aren't you?" they could hear her saying.

"So sorry to interrupt, Charlie," Grandad said to the customer, "but, Elsie, I think I'm going to take Tilly and Oskar for a trip into town to the British Library." He winked theatrically at Grandma, who shook her head slowly. "To see Amelia. You know, maybe . . ."

"Thank you, Archie. I've caught your drift, so you can stop winking." Grandma looked at Tilly and smiled, although it was laced with something Tilly couldn't quite identify. She handed Charlie a paper bag and receipt with a smile and then turned her attention fully to Tilly.

"It's very exciting, sweetheart," Grandma said. "And Oskar as well, you said? Archie, do you want to take over here and maybe Tilly and I can go and have a quick catch-up in the kitchen?"

Tilly nodded in a dazed silence, not quite able to wrap her head around her grandparents talking so casually about what seemed to be actual magic.

Over a cup of tea at the kitchen table, Grandma watched Tilly carefully.

"I'm sure you've already told Grandad all of this, but I'd love to hear about when you first realized what was happening."

"I didn't really realize until just now," Tilly said. "I didn't know what was happening to me, and when I first told Oskar he thought I was imagining things because I felt sad about Mum after finding those books of hers."

"I'm sorry we didn't tell you earlier, Tilly," Grandma said. "It's something we talked about a lot, but we decided that there was no way of explaining it before it actually happened; you would have thought we were going mad."

"I just can't believe I have magical grandparents and I didn't know!"

Grandma laughed. "Oh, Tilly. To my eternal sadness we are

not magical at all; we're just lucky enough to be able to use the natural magic of books and reading. It exists for everyone, but some of us can exert a little more control over it. I can no more cast a spell than I can convince your grandad to stop hoarding shoeboxes. So, where have you been so far? I hope it was somewhere particularly enjoyable and not too perilous?"

"I went to the tea party in *Alice in Wonderland* first, and then to school with Anne Shirley," Tilly said, feeling like she was reading lines from someone else's story, not talking about her own life. "Before I knew I could go inside books, when I'd just met Anne and Alice at Pages & Co., I tried to get Sara to come out of *A Little Princess,* but nothing happened."

"Why *A Little Princess*?" Grandma asked slowly.

"I'm not sure, it just felt like the right book," Tilly said. "It feels like ages since I read it, but Grandad had just told me it was my mum's favorite, and it reminded me how much I liked Sara."

"He did, did he?" Grandma said. "Well, I suppose that's true, but she liked a great many books apart from that one. And, if you didn't yet know what was possible, I'm not surprised nothing happened. When everything first kicks in it's only the characters you have the very strongest relationships with that tend to start popping up—it's why Anne and Alice ended up visiting you in Pages. Now, tell me what happened with Oskar."

So Tilly told Grandma everything that had happened over the last few days, right up to Oskar getting yanked into Avonlea with her and them confronting Grandad.

"And that brings us to here," Tilly concluded. "Grandad says we have to go and visit a librarian at the British Library."

"Well, it's sort of nearby the British Library," Grandma said. "But this is a bit of a special library, and a bit of a different librarian. Different but wonderful, and it's brilliant that you get to share it all with Oskar. It's good to have a friend around in this sort of situation."

"You mean the sort of situation where you find out you live in a magical bookshop and you can talk to your favorite characters?" Tilly said, a flicker of excitement starting to glow inside her.

"Exactly," Grandma said, smiling.

16

Welcome to the Underlibrary

"Archie and Tilly!" Mary said, delighted to see them when they pushed through the café door a few hours later. Oskar was buzzing excitedly by her side. "How lovely to have a visit. Sit down, sit down, and let me get you a pot of tea. Oskar says you've offered to take him into town with Tilly—are you sure it's not an imposition?"

"No time for tea, thanks, Mary," Grandad said. "And yes, of course, happy to have him along! Give them both a change of scenery, you know."

"Oh yes," Mary said, looking pleased, "it would be good for Oskar to get out for a bit and experience some culture at the same time. Is there an exhibition on at the moment that you fancied?"

Grandad faltered and Oskar jumped in. "It was something to do with *Alice in Wonderland* that you were keen on, wasn't it?"

"Yes, I believe you can see some of Lewis Carroll's manuscripts in the Treasures Gallery," Grandad bluffed.

Tilly and Oskar nodded along.

"Lovely," Mary said. "Thanks so much, Archie. Oskar, do you have your Oyster card?"

Oskar patted his jeans pocket in response.

"Perfect," Mary said. "Can't wait to hear all about it."

The trio set off for the station, which was only a five-minute walk down the high street. They scanned their cards on the machines and bundled onto a train heading into central London; Tilly spotted one person with a Harry Potter book, but people were mainly reading the free newspapers.

The British Library was a couple of minutes down the road from King's Cross station, but Oskar and Tilly still had to break into an awkward half-jog to keep up with Grandad, who was striding ahead, weaving speedily in and out of people wearing suits, and tourists wielding Tube maps and cameras. They nearly crashed into the back of him as he suddenly stopped outside a huge red-brick arch that marked the entrance.

"The British Library" was carved into the stone above their heads, and a black iron grid of letters spelled out the same words underneath it. They stepped through into a large courtyard full of every kind of person you could imagine: students with unwashed hair, weighed down by threadbare tote bags full of books; slick-looking businesspeople shaking hands, and hipsters with slim laptop cases and reusable coffee mugs all mingled around them. The floor of the courtyard was a grid of red and white bricks, and the coppery buildings that surrounded them were lined with red accents. The spires and clock tower of King's Cross station peeped out from behind the library walls, and a huge statue of a man holding some kind of mathematical equipment dominated the view.

"Who's that supposed to be?" Oskar asked, pointing at the vast sculpture.

"That's Sir Isaac Newton," Grandad said. "The statue was made by a sculptor called Eduardo Paolozzi. It's inspired by a drawing of Newton by William Blake, the writer."

"Awesome," Oskar breathed.

Grandad shepherded them toward the steps up to the main entrance. They passed the line of people having their bags checked by security guards and walked into a huge, airy entrance hall. There was a gift shop to their left, and a low white desk immediately in front of them where people were being given directions and information. Stairs and escalators led off in several directions and the air was filled with a gentle musical hum of noise and typing. It smelled like coffee and paper. Behind the reception desk was a huge tower made of glass and black metal that stretched up toward the ceiling, and which was lined with thousands upon thousands of ancient-looking books. Grandad headed straight toward it.

On the first floor there was a set of padded black doors with a gilt sign overhead saying "The King's Library." A narrow walkway led to a door behind a gate that said very clearly in large letters "Staff Only." Grandad pushed it open without hesitation.

"Uh, Grandad, it says staff only in here. I don't think we're allowed," Tilly said nervously.

"Don't worry, Tilly, it's okay. You'll see . . ." Grandad said, not seeming to notice the curious glances from the people working at the nearby desks. There was a black keypad by the door that Grandad punched four numbers into before pushing one of the heavy doors open with a satisfying click. Tilly and Oskar slipped through after Grandad into a cool, dark space lined with countless books. When she wasn't looking directly at them Tilly could have sworn the page edges were rustling and whispering to one another.

Grandad led them down a twisting metal staircase to what looked like a lift door tucked away in a corner. There was an "Out of Order" sign pinned up, but Grandad pressed the button anyway and the doors slid open.

Tilly and Oskar looked at Grandad in confusion, but he pushed them gently inside.

"Most of the British Library is four levels under your feet," Grandad said, "but, um, we sort of borrow some of the space from them."

"Who's we?" Tilly said, looking at him quizzically.

"You're about to find out," he said as he swiped some sort of card down a slot and pressed one of the buttons. The lift juddered and started to move, but, instead of going up or down, the now familiar toasty, marshmallowy smell filled the air and the sides of the lift cascaded down like wallpaper strips peeling away. In place of the beige walls there was an ornate interior made of dark, shiny wood and gilt decorations. Lines of gold buttons stretched from the floor to the very top of the lift, too high for Tilly to have pushed if she wanted to.

The doors pinged open.

"Welcome to the British Underlibrary," Grandad said. "After you."

17

Legere Est Peregrinari

Tilly and Oskar looked at each other in confusion. Grandad's tone had implied something huge and grand, but they were standing in a narrow corridor with wooden floorboards and nondescript doors lining the walls that curled round into darkness. It was far from unpleasant, but the majestic towers of books that they'd come from were much more impressive and Tilly had grown used to book magic transporting her somewhere wild and wonderful.

"Where did you say we were exactly?" she asked, looking up at Grandad.

"The Underlibrary," Grandad repeated, gesturing.

"Do you know something I don't?" Oskar said to Tilly under his breath. Tilly shook her head in response and he elbowed her into another question.

"What exactly is the Underlibrary?" Tilly asked. "We did the whole flippy magic thing in the lift, but we're just in a normal corridor. Ohhh . . . Are we in a normal corridor that is actually in a book?"

"What book is there an underlibrary in?" Oskar whispered to Tilly.

"No, no." Grandad was flustered and frustrated. "The Underlibrary is not from a book. This normal corridor is where all the 'flippy magic'—as you so casually put it, Matilda—comes from. Perhaps you'd better follow me."

Grandad set off down the corridor and Tilly and Oskar followed. Tilly was so focused on keeping up with Grandad that it wasn't until Oskar nudged her and pointed to one of the doors they were passing that she realized some of the signs were a little out of the ordinary. In between "Accounts" and "HR" they passed "The Map Room," "Classifications," and "Character Registry," and all the signs were prefaced by a string of numbers and dots. It didn't look much like either the calm, modern British Library upstairs or the cozy, friendly public library down the road from Pages & Co.

Eventually the corridor ended in a set of wooden double doors with twisty carved handles.

"Let's try this again," Grandad said, and pushed them open.

"That's more like it," Oskar said as he stepped into a room that was exactly what you might hope a secret, magical library would look like. The ceiling was painted deep turquoise and billowed high above them, cradled by ornate wooden arches. The floor was also wooden and the sound of their tapping heels

echoed around them, mixed in with hushed conversations and the whispering of pages being turned. They had entered through a door that was set into one of the narrow ends of the rectangular hall. The wall that faced them was painted cream and hung with wooden panels covered in gold writing above double doors that mirrored the ones they had just come through. Between the two sets of doors five floors of long aisles lined with shelves and shelves of books opened out into the main atrium. Each aisle ended with an ornate metal grille. The central atrium was empty of furniture apart from a large, circular desk in the very middle, which was looped round a huge wooden box made up of hundreds of tiny drawers with gold handles. Carved into the front of the desk were the words

"Legere est Peregrinari."

"What does that mean?" Tilly said, pointing.

"It's Latin," Grandad explained. "It doesn't have an easy English translation, but the verb *peregrinor* means to travel about, to roam or to wander, so it essentially means 'to read is to wander.' It's the motto of the Underlibrary."

The hall was full of people wearing navy blue cardigans with a gold trim. There were people carrying books and files, groups of them talking in small huddles, and Tilly glimpsed even more on the floors that stretched away from the hall, writing at long wooden desks. There was a cluster of librarians nearby, sorting and loading piles of books into an elaborate paternoster, like a giant dumbwaiter system. But, instead of the plain metal boxes

Tilly had seen being used to deliver food in restaurants, this was a large, intricate selection of wooden caskets hung together on coppery chains being hauled up and down and sideways, and being sent off to different floors of the library as they watched. Every few seconds the sound of peaceful chatter was interrupted by a thump as a man at the main desk stamped a book and threw it into a chute behind him.

"Okay, enough gawping for now; you'll have a chance to see more of it at some point, I promise. Let's go and find the Librarian," Grandad said, gently poking Tilly in the back to get her moving. Oskar followed, his mouth still open in wonder. They walked over to the desk in the middle, and the young man who looked up as they approached wore an easy smile on his face until he saw Grandad.

"Oh! Mr. . . . P-Pages," he stuttered. "I don't think we were expecting you?"

"No, I doubt you were," Grandad said, studiously avoiding Tilly's gaze. "Is Amelia around?"

"I don't know, sir. She'll probably be in her office. Shall I get someone to take you up?"

"I know the way," Grandad said, smiling gently at the man who was now nervously straightening his glasses.

"Oh yes, of course you do," he said sheepishly. "Can I let anyone else know you're here, sir?"

"That won't be necessary, thank you," Grandad said quickly. "Let's go, kids." He ushered them past the desk, where several of the people were now openly staring at them, and toward the doors at the opposite end of the hall. As they left the main atrium Tilly looked back over her shoulder to see that every single cardiganed person in the room had stopped in their tracks and was watching them leave.

"Grandad, why is everyone staring?" Tilly asked tentatively.

"Don't be silly, darling—they're just excited by visitors. This way, come on."

The trio were in another long corridor lined with wooden doors, although this time they were not named but numbered. Grandad counted under his breath until he reached number forty-two, then stopped abruptly. This time Tilly and Oskar did plow into the back of him.

"Here we are," he said, and knocked sharply on the door. It opened to reveal a woman with very straight, long, black hair and brown skin whose eyes widened at the sight of Grandad before her face broke into a broad and sincere smile.

"Archie Pages. It's been a while. Come in," she said, standing back to let them enter. They walked into a large, cozy, but decidedly normal office, not that dissimilar to the head teacher's office at school. A crumpled cardigan was hanging off the back of a chair behind a desk piled high with books and papers, and a very new-looking computer.

"Amelia, this is Oskar Roux, a friend, and Matilda Pages, my granddaughter."

An expression that Tilly couldn't quite read swept across

Amelia's face before she smiled and held out her hand to them. A large gold key on a chain round her neck swung as she leaned toward them.

"Welcome to the British Underlibrary. I'm Amelia Whisper, Librarian. Pleased to meet you."

Amelia gestured toward a collection of worn but comfortable-looking armchairs clustered in the corner of the office. She shrugged her cardigan on as they sat down, and Tilly noticed that there was an ornate key embroidered in gold thread on the breast of the cardigan alongside the same Latin words they'd seen in the main hall.

"You'll see that not much has changed, Archie," she said. "Cup of tea, anyone?"

Tilly nodded a yes please. "You've been here before, Grandad?" she asked.

Amelia laughed. "Well, of course he's been here before. The Librarian can hardly work from home."

"But you're the Librarian," Oskar said, confused.

"Right, I'm the Librarian now. But it used to be Tilly's grandad . . ." She faltered. "You didn't know?"

"No, Amelia, they didn't know. After everything that happened, Elsie and I decided it was for the best to start afresh—for Tilly's benefit," Grandad said.

Several emotions flickered across Amelia's face. "Well, I suppose that's your decision, Archie," she said in the end.

Oskar and Tilly exchanged a confused look.

"Can I just ask—?" Tilly started, but Grandad and Amelia kept talking.

"I need to sit down with you at some point and talk about Enoch too," Grandad was saying.

"Who's Enoch?" Oskar whispered to Tilly.

"I think he's Mr. Chalk," Tilly said.

"Would you mind not whispering while we're talking?" Grandad said much more sharply than usual.

"But we don't know anything!" Tilly said, stung by Grandad's tone. "You keep mentioning all these secrets and things and people, and I have no idea what is going on, and you just suddenly bring us to this *hidden, magical underground* library and expect us to be quiet and nod along and drink tea and YOU HAVEN'T EXPLAINED ANYTHING."

Oskar scuffed his heels together awkwardly and Amelia became very focused on her cup of tea.

Grandad looked at Tilly as though his heart had just cracked open.

"I'm sorry," he said. "This can wait, Amelia. Matilda, Oskar—I suppose we should start at the beginning."

18

Some Books Are Far Safer Than Others

"Bookwandering is the ability to travel inside books, and only a few readers can do it; you could say we can read a bit harder than most people. Something tips us over from visiting the books purely inside our imagination to being physically transported there. We still don't know precisely how it happens, and why bookwandering magic affects some people and not others. We think any reader probably has the potential to do it, but perhaps predictably there are very high numbers of booksellers or librarians, as bookwanderers almost always have a very special or particular relationship with books and reading. It's this intense relationship that first starts pulling characters out of books, and why your first bookwander is normally into a book you have an affinity with—which is why it's more unusual to find out that you were also able to travel into *Anne of Green Gables*, Oskar, even though you have never read it. Pulling characters out of their stories into the real world is actually more of a side effect, but it is almost always the way that we first realize someone has bookwandering abilities. And, as far as we can tell, bookwandering always takes place in a bookshop or library."

"So I pulled Anne and Alice out of their books without trying to?" Tilly asked.

"How come I haven't done that too?" Oskar said at the same time.

"I know you're going to have an awful lot of questions about this, but most of those questions will be covered in your induction session with one of the librarians, and I expect they'll be able to do it in a way that's more manageable, and enjoyable, than my fact-dumping. Actually—do you think we can squeeze one in today, Amelia?"

Amelia gave a small nod and went over to her desk and made a quiet phone call.

"They will be able to teach you how to control your bookwandering," Grandad went on. "The Underlibrary exists to protect readers, and our stories, and we have important rules in place to help do this. As I'm sure you can imagine, some books are far safer than others to explore, and we've had some pretty close calls in the past when people have pulled through all sorts of unsavory characters when their abilities awoke. Remind me to tell you about Gary and the orc one day.

"Now, as Amelia mentioned, I used to be the Librarian. I retired just after you were born, Tilly, as your grandma and I decided that with your mum not being around and us both getting older we would stay put at Pages & Co., especially as we didn't know whether you'd turn out to be a bookwanderer."

Amelia had now finished her phone call and was tapping her fingernails quietly but insistently on her desk. When Grandad paused she broke in.

"Archie. Do you think that—"

Grandad stopped her immediately and received a sharply raised eyebrow in response. "I realize that there is more to this story, but I think it best to let Tilly and Oskar get used to the basics first, don't you agree?" Grandad said, nodding his thanks.

"I want to hear the whole story," Tilly said instantly.

"This is just the basics?" Oskar said under his breath, shaking his head.

"I think you have more than enough to wrap your head around for now, Tilly. And, Amelia, if at all possible, I would appreciate you letting the other librarians know that we're just going to let the Underlibrary and the idea of bookwandering sink in a bit with Tilly and Oskar before we go into any more details. There's nothing for you to worry about, sweetheart," he added to Tilly.

"She wasn't worried until you said that," Oskar interjected, earning a hard stare from Grandad.

"Could my mum bookwander?" Tilly asked quietly.

"She could, yes, love," Grandad answered.

Tilly couldn't tell if the cracks in her heart were getting a little wider, or healing ever so slightly.

"You're so much like her, Matilda. I don't want to make you feel like Harry Potter, but you really do have her eyes," Amelia said, and Oskar struggled to suppress a giggle.

"You knew her?" Tilly said.

"Why, yes, we actually went to university together. She would have so loved to hear about your first bookwander. Anyway, there will be time to reminisce soon enough. Let's go and find the Reference Librarian to get you two registered," she said, giving both Oskar and Tilly an encouraging nod.

They went back out into the long corridor and walked a few meters down to a door where the number was covered by a handwritten sign in spidery letters that read "By Appointment Only."

"Ignore that," Amelia said. "Much as he hates it, I am still his boss and definitely do not need an appointment to see him." She pushed the door open at the same time as knocking, and the others followed her into a room that was almost identical in shape and size to hers, but much more sparsely furnished and with walls covered with metal filing cabinets and shelves full of huge, uniformly sized books.

"I do not tolerate people opening my door without knock— Ah, good afternoon, Ms. Whisper. I see you have guests," an icy voice said.

"You," breathed Tilly as Enoch Chalk turned round to face them.

19

Getting Lost in a Good Book

Grandad nodded curtly at Chalk, who swept a handkerchief covered in what looked like soot into the top drawer of his desk and shut it firmly.

"Good to see you still in your old office, Enoch," Grandad said in a polite but chilly voice.

Chalk's face contorted into a twisted version of a smile. "Why, yes, Archibald. Still here, still Reference Librarian, as you well know. I like it very much here—less politics, fewer opportunities for things to go awry. You know how it is. As you can see Amelia is doing an admirable job."

Amelia coughed. "Well, as heartwarming as this reunion is, we're here on official business. Enoch, we need to get Matilda and Oskar registered as bookwanderers."

"Of course," he said, going to pull out one of the huge volumes on his shelves.

Tilly looked at Grandad in a panic. "He works here?"

she whispered, but Grandad was entirely focused on watching Chalk.

Tilly steeled herself. "Why are you here?" she croaked.

Everyone turned to look at her.

"What did you say, girl?" Chalk said.

Tilly swallowed and thought of the look of righteous indignation when Anne had cracked the slate over Gilbert's head. *Be brave . . .*

"I said, 'Why are you here?'" she repeated, her voice more even this time.

"Where else would I be?" Chalk replied. "This is my office."

"But wherever I've been in the last few days, you've been there too! Are you following me?" Tilly said, a little more fiercely again.

At this Amelia started. "When have you met Matilda before, Enoch? This is the first time Archie has brought her here."

Tilly jumped in before Chalk could reply. "We've met three times before! The first time when he came to visit Grandad in the shop and then twice inside books. He was in both of the books I visited."

Everyone stopped looking at Tilly and turned their heads toward Chalk.

"You stamped Tilly?" Amelia said quietly.

"A mere routine check, I assure you," Chalk said. "It was such a pleasant surprise to learn of her existence when I popped in to Pages & Co., and she clearly has bookwandering in her blood, so I thought no harm in a quick trace stamp to see if she'd encountered any characters yet."

"That's very . . . dutiful of you," Amelia said.

"You know my research interests lie in the earliest signs of bookwandering and the abilities of our younger wanderers," Chalk said, still calm. "With such potent genes as Matilda here has it seemed a waste not to monitor how her abilities were developing."

"It seems a slightly irregular use of stamping," Amelia said, tilting her head. "We'll come back to this, Enoch."

"What's stamping?" Tilly asked.

"It's something a Senior Librarian can use to access a book they do not physically have possession of," Amelia said. "But it's not something you need to worry about.

"And why did you visit Pages & Co. in the first place, Enoch?" Amelia turned her focus back to Chalk.

"I had a query I thought Archibald might be best placed to help with, but I'm afraid he was not."

"I really think, considering the circumstances, that you should have let me know in advance of your visit to Archie," Amelia said.

"I would remind you that, while you may be the Librarian, I am not required to have visits to bookshops approved in advance," he said coldly.

Amelia frowned and cleared her throat. "We will talk

about this more in private, Enoch, but now it's time to register Tilly and Oskar."

Chalk nodded his head a fraction and beckoned Tilly over and gestured to the ledger.

"Name?"

"Matilda Rose Pages."

"Age at first bookwander?"

"Eleven."

"Home bookshop?"

"Pages & Co., I suppose?" Tilly looked questioningly at Grandad, who nodded.

"Owner of said bookshop?"

"Archibald and Elisabeth Pages."

"You're done. And the boy next."

Amelia nodded encouragingly at Oskar.

"Name?" Chalk said.

"Oskar Lucas Roux."

"Age at first bookwander?"

"Eleven."

"Home bookshop?"

"Pages & Co. as well, I guess?" Oskar said, unsure.

"I think so too," Amelia said, and Grandad nodded.

"Owner of said bookshop?"

"You literally just wrote it down for Tilly," Oskar said.

Chalk waited.

"Archibald and Elisabeth Pages," Oskar said.

Chalk finished writing the details down, recapped his fountain pen, precisely replaced it in a groove on his desk, and closed the ledger. The others watched as he brushed the already completely clean front cover, stood up, and ceremoniously slid it back onto the shelf. Tilly was sure she caught Amelia rolling her eyes.

"Are all these books full of bookwanderers?" Tilly asked. "Why do you keep all these records?"

"Yes, they are," Amelia replied. "The Underlibrary has been operating for a very long time and we believe people have had the ability to bookwander since books were first invented. More importantly, we keep records so we can keep track. We can't have unmonitored readers wandering around important texts, and we can't have characters straying out of their assigned pages without our knowledge.

"And it's also a wonderful record of our history," Amelia added. "A family tree of readers."

"Are you in here?" Tilly asked shyly.

"Yes, of course!" Amelia said, pulling down a ledger from a top shelf and flicking through its pages. "Here we go!"

Oskar and Tilly peered over her shoulder and saw her details recorded just as theirs had been.

"Can we see yours too?" Oskar asked Chalk.

"No, you may not," he said. "It would be an invasion of privacy."

"Nonsense, Enoch," Amelia said, sounding exasperated.

"What harm can it do? It's wonderful that new bookwanderers want to see more of our history. What year would you have been registered?"

Two pink spots of rage flashed on Chalk's pale cheeks.

"I have no desire to share personal information with these two children."

Amelia sighed and let it go.

"I have a question," said Oskar, putting his hand up as though he was at school. "Would we be able to see ourselves in a book after we'd been inside? Can we go back to Pages and find ourselves in *Anne of Green Gables*?"

"Good question," Amelia said, smiling. "When you walk into a book it's one of usually thousands of copies of that book, and you can't do any lasting damage to it, whatever you do while you're inside. As soon as you leave, the story will revert to the original, and your actions while you were inside it won't affect anyone else's version of the book. We don't recommend straying too far from the original story when you are bookwandering, but it's not possible for you to permanently change a story that you didn't create. Apart from in the Source Library, of course, where—"

Chalk interrupted her. "That's classified information, Ms. Whisper."

"Not for bookwanderers, Enoch," Amelia replied. She pulled out the key that was on the chain round her neck. "There are only two of these keys in existence: this one here and the one that belongs to Mr. Chalk. They are the only way to access the Source Library, where a first edition of every book in English is kept. Two copies of every book are delivered upstairs to the British Library. One goes into their stocks, and one comes down to us via Julian, the librarian upstairs whose job it is to liaise between the two libraries. Once it's delivered it's stamped and cataloged as a Source and imbued with the protections and powers of one. Those editions are fiercely protected because, if you travel in *those* books, you risk permanently altering the stories inside for all readers to come. And not to mention the fact that those books are particularly potent, and the original characters in them have a permanency and power that other editions don't; it's very important we keep Source characters in, and readers out."

"And changing the story would be bad, right?" said Oskar.

"It would be a disaster, Oskar," said Amelia. "I'm sure I don't need to tell you two how powerful books are. Books can change minds and change worlds, open doors and open minds, and plant seeds that can grow into magical or even terrifying things. Stories are things to be loved and respected at the same time; never underestimate the power of them. It's why books are often casualties of censorship; those who ban or burn books are those who are scared of what can be found among their pages. But imagine what might happen if those people also knew there was a way to permanently

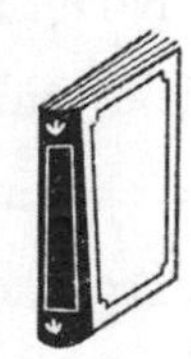

damage those stories; it's why we are so secretive. What we do could be put to such terrible use in the wrong hands."

"But regular bookwandering isn't dangerous, right?" Tilly asked nervously.

"I'm afraid it's not that simple," said Amelia. "Though the stories will always snap back to the original text once readers return to the real world, it gets a little bit more complicated while they are inside the story. As you'll know from visiting Avonlea, the world you are in is as real as it feels when you're reading it. You can touch things; you can eat and drink; you can interact with the story—however, that also means that you can get hurt, and even die. And, of course, there is always the danger of getting lost in a book. If you stay for too long, your knowledge of your real life starts to become hazy and time gets muddled. Although everything would come flooding back the moment you left, you run the risk of forgetting there is a real life to return to, not to mention you age unpredictably inside books. Stories enhance our lives; they shouldn't replace them.

"And that is just the good books; it's even easier to get lost in a bad book. Plot holes can be lethal."

Chalk shot Amelia a look, clearly growing impatient. "Much as it's delightful for me to listen to this, do you think you could take your personal conversations outside my office?"

"Come on then, we won't intrude on Mr. Chalk's time or carpet any longer. Any other questions you have will be answered in your induction," Amelia said. "Let's go and see if Sebastian has time to do that for you now."

Chalk watched them leave in silence before shutting the door firmly enough for it to be categorized as a slam, if you were paying attention, which no one really was anymore.

20

The Absolute Safest Books You Can Travel Into

Grandad, Amelia, Tilly, and Oskar walked back into the main hall, which was still a flurry of activity. A librarian came up to Amelia and talked quietly into her ear. Tilly pressed close to Grandad, trying to hear what the woman was saying, but she couldn't make it out.

"Thanks, Maddy," was all Amelia said in response, and the other librarian peeled off from their group as Amelia led them to a grand staircase in the middle of one of the long walls. The steps were made of marble and had ornate copper banisters leading up all five floors. They trooped up several flights of steps and emerged on the fourth floor, which was lined with tall shelves of books. One end opened out onto the hall, where some of the boxes of books Tilly and Oskar had seen being loaded downstairs were sliding onto a pulley system and being emptied by two librarians; the other end was lined with mirrors, making the room look like it stretched out endlessly.

There were several upright burgundy-leather chairs surrounding an oval wooden table, which had a brass and green glass lamp at its center. A very neatly dressed man who wore his cardigan with a white shirt and bow tie came to greet them.

"Ms. Whisper, a pleasure," he said, pushing the bridge of his black glasses farther up his nose and bobbing his head in a deferential bow of sorts. "Are these our new bookwanderers?"

"Hi, Seb, yes. Sorry for the lack of notice, but do you have time for an induction, even if it's just the abridged version? This is Oskar Roux, and this is Matilda Pages. And this is her grandfather, Archie Pages."

Seb started at Grandad's name, but quickly composed himself and held out his hand to Grandad, who shook it firmly. "Good to meet you, sir. And thrilled to have you among our ranks, Oskar and Tilly. Happy to fit you in for an induction, of course. You've saved me from my cataloging. Take a seat." He gestured to the leather armchairs and table.

"Do you need us to stay, Seb?" Amelia asked. "Archie and I have a lot to catch up on, if you can spare us?"

"We'll be absolutely fine here," Seb replied. "I'll get one of the others to come and get you when we're finished. I imagine these two are naturals anyway."

"Thanks, Seb," Amelia said, touching Grandad's elbow gently to motion him to leave.

Tilly looked at him, feeling a little panicked by how quickly everything had escalated over the last few hours.

"You're safe here, Tilly," Grandad reassured her. "Seb can come and get me if you need anything at all and I'll just be downstairs in Amelia's office. Have fun. Listen carefully."

When Grandad and Amelia had left, Seb sat down with Oskar and Tilly at the wooden table, smiling encouragingly.

"So, when did you chaps first realize you could bookwander?" he asked, smoothing his cardigan down.

"Well, Anne—you know, from *Anne of Green Gables*—first appeared in the bookshop last week, but we only found out it was called bookwandering about an hour ago," Tilly said.

"Goodness, rather a baptism of fire, as the saying goes," Seb said, smiling. "Nothing to worry about; we can take things nice and steady. We don't need to run before we can walk. I'm here to answer all your questions and let you practice in a safe, controlled environment. Is there anything you want to know before we start? I'm unsure what you've been told so far."

Tilly and Oskar sat in stunned silence for a moment, wondering where to begin.

"How come I never saw any characters in the real world but I could follow Tilly into *Anne of Green Gables*?" Oskar asked.

Seb looked startled. "You followed Tilly into a book? Are you sure? I've only heard of that happening once in a blue moon."

"Yes, Anne took us both in at the same time, even though I couldn't see her in the shop and we all . . . wandered? Appeared? Okay, actually I have a new question." Oskar interrupted his own train of thought. "Are we talking about magic here?"

Seb smiled again. "In short, yes. We are talking about book magic. Bookwandering is, at its core, the magic of books and imagination pushed to its limit, and then tipped over a little bit farther. There are millions of readers across the world and throughout time who have loved books, who can vividly imagine their favorite scenes and characters, who have real and important relationships with books, but there are only a handful of us who can wander. I'm afraid there aren't any spells or magic words, and limited numbers of dragons and witches, but we are definitely dealing with magic."

"I figured," Oskar said.

"You seem very relaxed about all of this," Tilly said. She did not feel relaxed about anything she had learned over the last hour or so.

"Well, now it's happened, I'm glad to have some explanations for it, you know?" Oskar said. "It would be way worse if no one had been able to tell us what was going on, right?"

"I guess so," Tilly said, unconvinced. "Hang on. Can we just go back to you saying there were *limited* numbers of dragons and witches? Why aren't there *no* dragons and witches?"

"Well, if you visit a book with dragons and witches, you will encounter dragons and witches in the book," Seb said. "A key part of what I need you to understand is that the things you come across in books are very real if you are inside a book. A dragon is a dragon is a dragon. Some books are more dangerous than others. In fact, that's part of the reason we use these books for practicing," he said, dropping a pile of slim, colorful books onto the table. "We're going to start with the basics; it's vital you learn how to control when you bookwander and how to get in and out when you want. You should hear some of the ancient librarian stories about people getting stuck . . ." He tailed off and swallowed awkwardly. "But we have the Archivists if things go really wrong."

"The Archivists?" Tilly repeated.

"They're sort of like the United Nations of bookwandering. Every country has its own Underlibrary, but then above them there are the Archivists. I've never even seen them, and I believe the Archive itself moves locations—but theoretically they're brought in if things get out of hand. Honestly, I sometimes wonder if they're a bit of an old wives' tale themselves: no one here has ever had to deal with them as far as I know. Anyway."

He pushed the books toward them.

Tilly picked one up. "*Things We Like*," she read from the front cover.

Oskar picked up another one. "*Play with Us*," he read. "These look like the books we had in primary school, the ones we learned to read from."

"That's exactly what they are," Seb said. "These are the absolute safest books you can travel into." He took *Play with Us* from Oskar and handed it to Tilly. "Okay, Tilly, you're going to go first as your bookwandering seems to be slightly more typical so far."

Oskar grimaced.

"Don't worry, we'll get you sorted out," Seb reassured him. "Okay. The primary rule of bookwandering is that you must keep the copy of the book with you when you travel—"

"But I didn't have a book with me when I went into *Alice in Wonderland* or *Anne of Green Gables*," Tilly interrupted.

"You were with a character from the book. Characters can take you in, and bring you out, and, in fact, we find that if you bookwander with a character, they have a lot more control than if you wander in by yourself. If you do wander in by yourself, characters will believe you to be part of the story, even if your presence is quite inexplicable. They may wonder why you are in a particular place, but they won't question your fundamental existence. But if a character pulls you into their story, like Anne did to you from Pages & Co., they will remember where you are really from. Anne knew that you and Oskar weren't part of her book, did she not? But no one else did?"

Tilly nodded.

"We actually discourage that style of travel as you are reliant on the character to get you out again, and it's not always obvious, without a tracking stamp, which copy of the book you're in."

"Oh," Tilly said, her face scrunching in sadness. "Does that mean that Anne wouldn't remember me if I went into *Green Gables* by myself?"

"I'm afraid not," Seb said. "But we don't have much time, so shall we begin?" He leaned across the table and flicked through the opening pages, which were glossaries of vocabulary, and on to the first page, which was a drawing of a boy holding a basketball, with the word "Peter" on the opposite page. "So, first of all, I'm going to ask you to read the whole book; it will only take you a few minutes. You can bookwander without doing this first, but it will get your imagination into gear, and the better you know a story, the safer you'll be inside. Oskar, you may as well read the other one too at the same time—kill two birds with one stone and all. Just read as you normally would."

Tilly and Oskar exchanged a skeptical glance, but Seb nodded them on, so they turned to their books. It took them only two or three minutes to read them. They were so simple and short. The two of them looked up expectantly at Seb.

"When you read yourself into a book you read yourself into a specific moment. If you start at the start, you will travel to the start, etc. You have control over where you visit. You should never travel to within ten pages of the end of a book."

"Why not?" Oskar asked.

"Endings are unpredictable," Seb explained. "It is possible to visit the end of a book—in fact, many have tried in order to visit their favorite battles, or weddings, or deaths—but you need to be poised to return at the snap of a finger, and until you are much more experienced we would ask you not to risk it."

"Why is it more dangerous? What happens?" Tilly asked.

"If you don't time it just right, you can get rather stuck in the Endpapers," Seb said.

"Sorry, what are 'endpapers'?" Oskar asked.

"No need to apologize," Seb said. "*Lowercase* endpapers are the leaves at the very beginning and end of a book, sometimes stuck to the inside of the cover. *Uppercase* Endpapers are the negative matter at the end of books that acts as a sort of cushion to bounce characters back if something goes wrong, so we can find them and put them back into their stories. It's a safety net for characters, not for readers. It's a theoretical nothing space for readers. The story has ended, but you're still in the book, and it can be very tricky to get back from there–the usual rules don't apply."

"There are a lot of rules," Oskar muttered.

"There are a lot of risks," said Seb. "Remember, this isn't a game, Oskar. We're trying to keep you safe. Okay, pay attention: this bit is important," Seb went on, straightening his glasses. "To get back out of a book you must reread the last line, from the same copy of the same book."

"And we won't get stuck in the Endpapers that way?" Tilly asked.

"An excellent question, Tilly, but no," Seb replied. "If you read the last line, it's as if you're inserting your own full stop, or typing 'The End.' It works like a command, an instruction. The Endpapers are where you'll wind up if you're wandering near the end of a book and you let it finish without you leaving. But it's nothing to worry about—just make sure you stick to reading the last line and you'll be fine. A book will return you safely to whichever bookshop or library you read yourself in from."

"But what happens if you're reading at home?" Oskar said. "Would it take you home?"

"Bookwandering is only possible in bookshops and libraries in our experience. It just doesn't seem to work unless you are in a book emporium of some kind; you need the potency of all the different book worlds brought together in one space."

Seb sat back with a dreamy look on his face. "You know when you walk into a bookshop and you see all those thousands of books lined up in front of you? That intoxicating feeling of knowing that behind each cover is a different world to explore, like thousands of tiny portals? That adrenaline rush just before you open a new book? The thrill of being surrounded by fellow book lovers? That is what fuels bookwandering, and it comes to life in bookshops."

21

Time Works Differently in Books

Oskar interrupted Seb's bookish reverie with a cough, bringing him back down to earth.

"Anyway, sorry, back to business. Tilly, do you want to have a go at reading yourself into the book?" He flipped it open flat at a page that read: *Here is a toyshop.*

Tilly picked it up apprehensively. "So I just read it? Like normal? Hang on, how come I haven't accidentally read myself into a book before?"

"Well, you might have felt the first stirrings of the ability before, without knowing what you were feeling. Have you ever lost track of time because you were so involved in a book? Or looked up and it's taken you a few seconds to realize where you are? When you stop being distracted by what's going on around you and you're reading without thinking about the process of reading? That's your brain, and your heart, starting to sync with the story. But you have to read with intent to bookwander; you won't ever fall into a story by accident, even if you're still getting to grips with how it all works.

"We don't really know why different people's abilities kick in at different times; it often happens at about your age as you start to really develop your own individual relationship with books and find your favorites. There also seems to be a correlation with times of change or upset; we think it might be that while you're occupied with other things it gives the magic inside you a chance to spill out. And, once magic has revealed itself, it's very hard to ignore. Bookwandering is naturally in you, Tilly. Don't worry about getting it right or wrong. The important thing is that you know it's possible, because you've done it with Alice and Anne, so just focus on the story, and read the line . . . And remember to keep hold of the book."

"What happens if I can't get back? I read the last line and nothing happens? What if I lose the book? Are you sure I should be doing this?"

"None of that will occur, but I can pull you out, if need be. That copy of the book is tethered to the Underlibrary, but it's also been registered as a training book so its borders are more flexible and I can come and get you. There are lots of systems the library has in place to allow us to find and help wanderers, but believe me, it won't come to that. Now, break a leg, as they say in the theater."

Tilly nodded and took a deep breath. She tried to cut off everything going on around her and simply read. It took her a fraction of a second to read the simple sentence, but instantly that smoky, sweet smell started to billow around her, and the walls of reality began to fold down on themselves. Instead of a fully realized world, all she could see was white. It was like standing in a room full of dense white fog; there were no sounds, or smells, just white.

Tilly started to panic and realized that she had no idea how to contact Seb if something went wrong, but at that moment a silky red setter seemed to come from nowhere and bounded past her. She turned as the dog passed and saw that the toyshop from the book had sprung up behind her. It had turquoise walls with big windows framed in yellow. The windows were stuffed full of all kinds of old-fashioned-looking toys: dolls in frothy, lacy dresses; plastic cars; teddy bears; and even a rocking horse. The only thing to do seemed to be to follow the dog in through the open door. Inside, a woman in a purple shirt was behind the till, talking to a boy in an orange jumper holding a huge digger toy. A blonde girl in a pink turtleneck was pointing at a doll in a glass case, and the dog was snuffling at a toy dog in the corner.

"Hello?" Tilly said tentatively as she went in.

Both children looked up at her, but the dog kept sniffing the toy dog.

"Here is Peter," the girl said, pointing at the boy.

"Here is Jane," the boy replied, pointing at the girl.

"Nice to meet you. I'm Tilly," she said, giving an awkward half-wave.

"I like Peter," Jane said.

"I like Jane," Peter said.

"Great," Tilly said. "How come there's nothing outside the toyshop?" she asked.

"Here is a toyshop," said Peter.

"I like the toyshop," said Jane.

"Sure, me too," said Tilly. "It's a nice toyshop. Is that your dog?"

"Peter likes the dog," said Jane.

"Jane likes the dog," said Peter.

"Okay then," Tilly said. "I guess we all like the dog."

The woman behind the counter didn't say anything.

"Well, this is creepy," Tilly said under her breath. "Am I allowed to leave yet?" She flicked the book to the last page and read, "*Here is Peter in the tree. Peter has the ball.*" There was a horrible moment when nothing appeared to happen before the toyshop dissolved around her and was replaced by the solid, book-lined walls of the library.

Seb gave her a big thumbs-up, and Oskar looked amazed. "You were only gone for, like, seconds!" he said.

"Time works differently in books," Seb explained. "You know how in books swathes of time just get missed out? A new chapter starts 'the next day' or even 'the next week' and you don't really know what's happened before then? Or the time it takes to describe something is even longer than how long it would actually take?" Oskar and Tilly nodded. "You'll be away from the real world for roughly how long it would take you to read the passage, even if it feels longer when you're inside, but it can be unpredictable, I'm afraid."

Seb pushed the other book toward Oskar.

"Okay, your turn. Do you feel comfortable having a go? Obviously we're not quite so sure how your bookwandering is going to manifest, but I feel happy enough that you have the core ability required because of your adventures in Avonlea, and, as I said to Tilly, this is a training book and I can come and—"

But Seb's reassurances were interrupted by a stern-looking librarian with a sharp goatee, and wearing a black cardigan edged with silver, emerging from the stairs. He looked at Tilly and Oskar with barely masked curiosity.

"Sorry to interrupt, Sebastian, but could you come and assist with something that's arisen downstairs? A new bookwanderer has got into a situation in *Peter Pan* and we're hoping it's a simple administrative error you can unpick more efficiently than us."

Seb tutted, but got to his feet.

"It can't wait?"

"Ideally not," the librarian said. "He seems to have lost a lost boy."

Seb sighed and turned to Tilly and Oskar. "You two need to stay here, do you understand me? Do not move. I will return soon or I'll find your grandad and he'll come and retrieve you." He turned and looked at them over the top of his glasses. "Stay. Here."

Oskar and Tilly nodded as Seb followed the other librarian

downstairs. They watched him over the banister as he joined a couple of librarians whose cardigans were also black and edged with silver. They were all walking briskly toward the circular main desk on the ground floor. The first one to reach it swung open a door in the side of the wooden chest of drawers and disappeared inside.

"They're really into their fancy cardigans here, huh?" Oskar said. "What are we supposed to do while we wait? Should we go and find your grandad?"

"Seb told us to stay here. If they need Amelia to help with whatever's going on, then I'm sure he'll come and find us."

"I can't believe I didn't get a chance to bookwander," Oskar said. "No offense, but I think they should have started with me because they know you can do it, but I still don't know if I can do it without you."

"Seb will be back soon and you'll get to have a go. That book wasn't fun like visiting Avonlea anyway. It was weird and kind of dull. Where would you most like to go once we're allowed?" she asked.

"Hogwarts! Obvious choice," Oskar said. "I want to go to the Yule Ball, or maybe watch the dragon task from the Triwizard Tournament. Or meet Luna."

"But what if you ran into Voldemort? Or Umbridge?" Tilly said. "And I don't think we'd be able to do magic—we'd be Muggles."

"Well, what about Middle-earth?" Oskar suggested.

"Way too dangerous," Tilly said. "Orcs, trolls, giant spiders . . ." She checked the various monstrosities off on her fingers.

"Fine, fine," Oskar said. "Okay, how about Oxford in *The Golden Compass*?"

"I wouldn't want to run into the child snatchers," Tilly said.

"Ugh, why are books so dangerous?" Oskar said.

"I guess a book about a nice safe place where nothing happens would be kind of boring and no one would read it," Tilly said as Oskar wandered down the stretches of shelves, looking at the spines.

"A little bit of danger is okay, though, surely?" he said, holding up a book to show Tilly.

"*Treasure Island*? Are you sure? Isn't that all about pirates and, I don't know, death and betrayal and stuff?"

Oskar scrunched his nose up. "Kind of. There are definitely pirates, but most of them are pretty friendly from what I remember. It was a while ago I listened to the audiobook. We'll just make sure we read a bit where there's nothing dangerous happening." He started flicking through the pages as Tilly tried to ignore the slightly sick feeling in her stomach.

"Oskar, I'm not sure this is—"

But she was cut off as Oskar cracked the spine, grabbed her hand, and started to read.

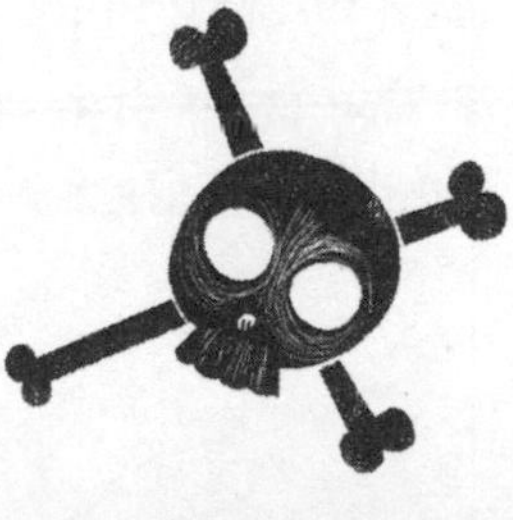

22

An Incredibly Bad Idea

"When I had done breakfasting the squire gave me a note addressed to John Silver, at the sign of the Spy-glass, and told me I should easily find the place by following the line of the docks and keeping a bright lookout for a little tavern with a large brass telescope for sign. I set off, overjoyed at this opportunity to see some more of the ships and seamen, and picked my way among a great crowd of people and carts and bales, for the dock was now at its busiest, until I found the tavern in question."

The comforting smell of paper, ink, and wood turned sweet and marshmallowy before transitioning into the much more pungent stink of fish, sweat, and the sea. Tilly wrinkled her nose as the Underlibrary d i s s o l v e d around them and was replaced by a bustling, smelly dock.

Oskar grinned. "See, nothing more dangerous than—" But at that moment a gruff-looking man covered in tattoos elbowed him in the side.

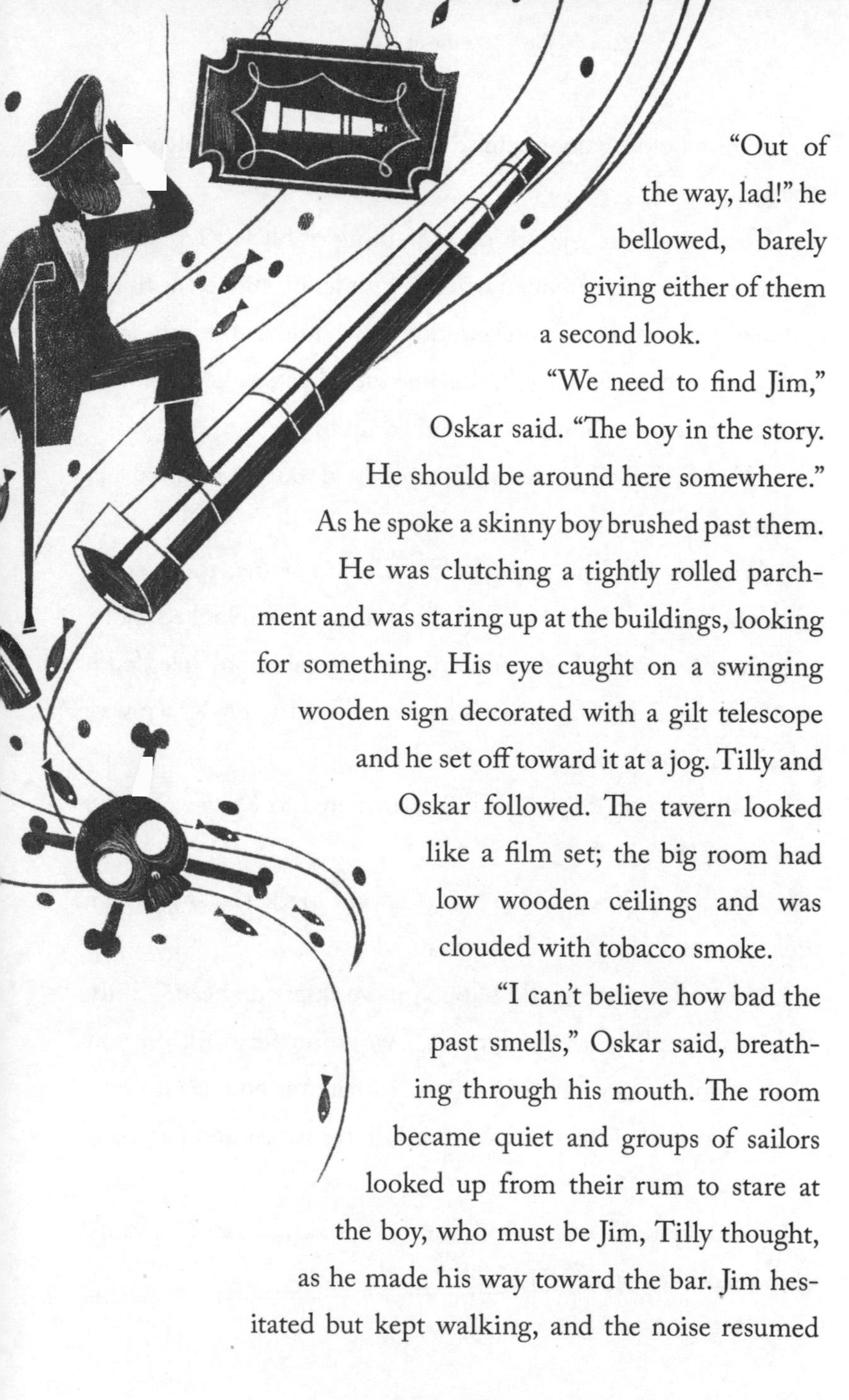

"Out of the way, lad!" he bellowed, barely giving either of them a second look.

"We need to find Jim," Oskar said. "The boy in the story. He should be around here somewhere."

As he spoke a skinny boy brushed past them. He was clutching a tightly rolled parchment and was staring up at the buildings, looking for something. His eye caught on a swinging wooden sign decorated with a gilt telescope and he set off toward it at a jog. Tilly and Oskar followed. The tavern looked like a film set; the big room had low wooden ceilings and was clouded with tobacco smoke.

"I can't believe how bad the past smells," Oskar said, breathing through his mouth. The room became quiet and groups of sailors looked up from their rum to stare at the boy, who must be Jim, Tilly thought, as he made his way toward the bar. Jim hesitated but kept walking, and the noise resumed around him before a door behind the bar swung open and a man emerged.

There was barely anything remaining of his left leg, and a carved wooden peg extended from just under his hip to the floor, matched by a wooden crutch under his shoulder. He was over six feet tall with a smiling, handsome face that was hard to look away from. Jim swallowed and walked up to him.

"Mr. Silver, sir?" he said, and held out the rolled-up parchment.

"Yes, my lad," he replied. "Such is my name, to be sure. And who may you be?" He read the note and then looked more intently at Jim. "Oh! I see. You are our new cabin boy; pleased I am to see you." He shook Jim's hand firmly. The boy's face was pale, but his back straight.

"What do we do now?" Tilly whispered to Oskar. "You've seen enough, right?"

"Not even close," Oskar said. "I want to see the ship. Let's stick around and try to follow them."

"I wonder what would happen if we skipped ahead?" Tilly said. "Try reading a later bit—can we jump forward, do you think? I don't fancy hanging around in here for hours."

Oskar pulled the book from inside his jacket and passed it to Tilly.

"You look—I won't find the bit quickly enough; I can't skim-read like you can," he said.

"But . . ."

"Seriously, you do it."

Tilly looked down the list of chapter titles.

"Okay, 'Chapter Ten: The Voyage'—sound about right?" She took Oskar's arm and started to read. The air around them fizzed and fuzzed, but instead of finding themselves back outside on the dock they were standing deep in the creaking innards of the ship itself, in a lavishly decorated room with a huge desk at its center covered by a large parchment map. The room was lined with bookshelves with pile upon pile of rolled-up maps tucked in between the spines.

"Uh, Tilly, I just wanted to see the ship from outside, you know," Oskar said. "I don't want to worry you, but we probably shouldn't stay here too long in case anyone sees us."

"I know, I know," Tilly said, flustered. "I don't know anything about this book—I thought this bit was describing them getting things ready to go on board. I should never have wandered into something I've not read; this was an incredibly bad idea."

"It's fine," Oskar said. "We can go anytime we want, remember? We just have to read the end of the book, like Seb said, and we'll go straight back to the Underlibrary. Pass it here." But as Oskar reached out to take the book from Tilly the wooden stairs in the corner of the room creaked and one black leather boot and one wooden peg appeared, followed by the man wearing them: Long John Silver.

"What have we here then?" he said, coming toward them, as Tilly held the book behind her back. "Two stowaways? I'm not sure you'll like where we're headed, laddies." He peered closer at Tilly. "A laddie *and* a lassie stowaway, are we? It's fiendish bad luck to have a woman on board, so the legends go—and in the captain's quarters as well?"

"Actually, sir," Oskar said, "we've sort of ended up here by accident, so, if you don't mind, we'll just get back off the boat."

Silver tipped his head back and laughed, revealing a few missing teeth. "Now how, might I ask, did you end up in our esteemed captain's private rooms accidentally?" He lurched closer. "Who asked you to hide away in here?"

"No one, I promise!" Tilly said. "We didn't realize these were the captain's rooms; we were just . . . we were just exploring because Oskar likes boats and, if you'd just let us off again, that would be great, thank you."

Silver stepped back. "Why, of course, milady, as you asked so politely. Allow me to take whatever you are holding there, to aid you on your way." Smiling, he offered an arm to Tilly and took the copy of *Treasure Island* in his other hand. "Let me accompany you to the deck."

Oskar eyed the book but shrugged at Tilly and followed them, unsure what other options they had. The ship rocked in the water as they made their way upstairs.

"Not got your sea legs yet, I see." Silver laughed as the boat rocked on the waves beneath them and Tilly wobbled against him. "Now, here we are. Just up there and you two can be off and back to your, what was it you said? Oh yes, your boat exploring." He smiled crookedly and bent into a sweeping bow. Tilly and Oskar clambered past him up the final steps to the deck to see the ocean stitched to the horizon, with no land in sight.

23

This Is Why You Should Always Follow the Rules

Tilly and Oskar looked at each other in horror as Silver laughed again.

"Now, milady," he said, bowing sarcastically in front of Tilly, "why don't you tell your old friend John exactly why you're aboard the *Hispaniola*, and why we found you rattling around in our noble Captain Smollett's rooms." He examined the book in his hand. "And why might you be borrowing this tome from his private bookshelves?"

He started when he saw the title of the book. "*Treasure Island*! An interesting book for you to have selected—what do you know of the isle of treasure? And I wonder what our captain knows of it to have this here book among his collection?"

Tilly and Oskar stayed silent. Neither of them had a clue how they might talk their way out of this.

"Not feeling talkative? Let me give you a little time to think while I consult with some of my associates about what to do with you. Might not be any need to involve the captain quite yet." He took each of them by the shoulder in a firm but painless grip and maneuvered them back down the steps. But instead of turning toward the captain's quarters he took them down another level into what was obviously the ship's kitchen.

"Welcome to my galley," Silver said. "I'm just going to ask you to wait here for a moment. But I'm a kind host, you'll see." He tossed them an apple each before he led them into a cupboard stacked with casks and locked the door behind them, taking the book with him.

Tilly took some deep breaths to try to calm down.

"What on earth are we going to do now?" she said to Oskar. "What happens if he reads the book and sees his own name in there? He doesn't know he's not real. Oh my goodness, it was such a bad idea to come here, Oskar. This is why you should always follow the rules."

Oskar crunched his apple loudly and Tilly looked at him, exasperated.

"No need to get hungry, is there?" he said.

"Okay, just give me a minute to think," Tilly said. They both stood with their backs against the rough wood wall, Oskar crunching and Tilly pressing her fingers to her temples in concentration.

"Okay. Okay. We just need to get the book back. That's all. If we can get the book, we can read ourselves out straightaway. So we just have to grab it as soon as we see it."

"I don't think that will go down very well," Oskar said. "He doesn't seem like a man who likes having his stuff grabbed, you know?"

"But if we read ourselves out immediately it doesn't matter if we make him cross. We just need to do it as quickly as possible. So, when he comes back—"

"Then what?" Silver said, opening the cupboard door.

"We were just hoping we could have our book back, Mr. Silver," Tilly said as politely as she could.

"I'm afraid that's not an option quite at this moment, my darlin'. Indeed, my friends are of the opinion that if you two aren't more forthcoming with some answers, then we'll have to enact a little sea justice. You understand it's not your old friend John's preferred manner of doing things, but sometimes it's important to uphold the illusion of democracy; we don't want a mutiny on our hands now, do we? Not over a book. In fact, as the captain has just retired for his afternoon brandy I'm going to take you upstairs to meet with some of them to see if you can satisfy their curiosity. If you'll follow me . . . And there's no point running off—very few satisfactory places to hide in for long on a ship." Silver smiled.

The deck was almost empty save for a small group of distinctly unsavory-looking men gathered in a huddle. Silver coughed and they turned to leer at Oskar and Tilly.

"Now, gentlemen, where's that book?" Silver said as they approached. A grimy man with a dirty rag tied over his eyes staggered forward with the book in his hand and Silver sighed. "Eyeless Horace. An enlightened choice to try to discern the secrets of the printed word. As always I see that the particulars of a plan rest on my shoulders."

"I couldn't read before I lost my eyes anyways," the man said.

"A tot of rum to the man who is useless twice over," Silver said sarcastically. "Lad, if you'd follow me this way." He took Oskar's arm in an iron grip and led him to the side of the boat, where a plank of wood stuck out over the water.

He turned to Tilly. "Now, lassie, I'm going to need to know why you ended up aboard the *Hispaniola* on this particular voyage and why you are in possession of a book about the isle of treasure. As elegant as we may seem we are not above a little encouragement to telling the truth," he said as one of the men unceremoniously picked up Oskar and put him on the plank. Silver smiled like a crocodile who'd spotted his dinner and leafed through the pages at a leisurely pace until all of a sudden his face drained of color and he stared closely at the page.

"What witchcraft is this, child?" he said quietly, thrusting the book in Tilly's face.

"What . . . what do you mean?" she stuttered.

"Don't play the innocent," he whispered, pointing to a page that quite clearly showed his name several times. "Where did you get this grimoire? Did Flint send you? Is the captain in on this?" Silver took a step toward her, forcing Tilly backward until she was pressed against the side of the boat where Oskar wobbled on the plank, trying desperately to keep his balance. "You have one more chance remaining, before you and your friend are dealt with once and for all. We may be pirates, but we'll not risk this vessel with sorcery." He took a last look at the book, then threw it overboard. In a split second Tilly knew there was only one option left.

"Jump!" she bellowed at Oskar and threw herself after the book and over the side of the *Hispaniola*. She hit the choppy water in an ice-cold splash that momentarily took her breath away. Her clothes were immediately soaked through as she thrashed around, desperately looking for the book. She saw it floating a few meters from her and launched into a front crawl toward it, waves slapping against her, rescuing it just as it started to become too waterlogged to stay on the surface.

Tilly gasped, and looked on in horror as Oskar wobbled on the edge of the plank. "You have to jump!"

"I can't swim!" he shouted down to her as one of the pirates climbed onto the other end of the plank.

"Oskar, you have to!" she shouted as she tried to find the last page of the book while kicking her feet to stay above the waves. "Aim for me!"

Oskar locked eyes with her and she nodded. He closed his eyes and launched himself off the end of the plank, arms and legs windmilling through the air as Tilly splashed toward him. He landed in the water with a huge splash as the pirates jeered from the boat. He surfaced but almost immediately started sinking again.

"We have to be touching!" Tilly yelled, holding her arm out. As Oskar's fingertips brushed hers she took a huge gasp of air and bellowed the last line of the book. *"Pieces of eight! Pieces of eight!"*

It was as if someone had pulled the plug of the ocean and suddenly Tilly could breathe properly again as the Underlibrary REBUILT ITSELF around them.

Oskar fell to his knees, coughing up water, while Tilly pressed her forehead against the wood of the wall, letting its reassuring warm solidness anchor her back to dry land. They both stood dripping on the carpet as Grandad appeared at the top of the stairs. Tilly kicked the nearly disintegrated copy of the book under the table.

"Why on earth are you both wet?" he asked.

"We fell in the sea," Oskar said without thinking.

"You fell in the sea? On your induction?" Grandad said.

"We, um, we landed in the wrong bit of the book," Tilly said.

"Honestly," Grandad muttered. "Sending new bookwanderers to scenes by the sea. Standards are obviously slipping; would never have happened in my day. Anyway, let's go. Goodness knows what we're going to say to your mum about the state of your clothes, though, Oskar."

Although they got several funny looks on the train home, by the time they were back at Pages & Co. Oskar's and Tilly's clothes were mostly dry, if lightly crusted with salt.

"Tilly, go and get changed, and see if you can find Oskar a clean T-shirt to wear," Grandad said. "We'll put these things through the wash while we're chatting."

Fifteen minutes later they were sitting round the kitchen table with Grandma putting mugs of hot chocolate and plates of toasted brioche with cherry jam in front of them. Oskar was wearing a T-shirt with the cover of *The Phantom Tollbooth* printed on it.

"So, how did it go?" Grandma asked gently.

"It was awesome," Oskar said, grinning.

"Why didn't you tell me before?" Tilly said. "Why didn't you tell me about bookwandering, and that Grandad was the Librarian? I thought you'd always lived here?"

"Well, we have lived here a long time," Grandma said. "This bookshop has been in my family for decades and I've been in charge since my mum died years ago."

"But why's Archie called Pages too?" Oskar asked.

"Because he took my name when we got married, the same way people often take each other's names," Grandma said.

"We wanted to keep the Pages name because of the bookshop's legacy," Grandad said. "Not to mention what bookseller or librarian wouldn't seize the chance of such a booky surname!"

"The history of this shop stretches way back," Grandma said.

"You come from a long line of booksellers, Tilly. Your family tree is full of them, as well as librarians and writers and readers; it's in your blood."

Oskar cleared his throat. "Uh, I think I'm going to go home now, and leave you guys to it for a bit," he said quietly, giving Tilly an awkward pat on the shoulder. "Thank you for taking me today, and thank you for the T-shirt; I'll bring it back tomorrow."

Grandma gave him a smile. "Do come round tomorrow and we can chat further, Oskar. I know you must have more questions. And I'm sorry to be blunt, but you know you can't tell your mum about this?"

"Like she'd believe me anyway," Oskar said.

24

Everything Has Tilted on Its Axis

After Grandad had seen Oskar to the door, the three of them settled down round the kitchen table in a slightly uneasy silence. Tilly was cycling through a whirlwind of different feelings and she didn't know where it would settle. She wasn't sure if she felt cross or excited or scared.

"I don't understand why you couldn't tell me sooner," she decided to begin with.

"I already explained at the Underlibrary," Grandad started to answer. "There are so many reasons that—"

"I would have believed you," Tilly interrupted.

"It's easy to feel like that now you know," Grandma said. "But try to imagine how you would have reacted if you had been told this before anything had happened to prove it to you."

"I would have believed you," Tilly repeated more firmly. "I hate secrets."

"I promise you we've kept as little as possible from you,"

Grandad said. "I know it feels like everything has tilted on its axis today, but we've always been honest with you about everything that isn't linked to bookwandering."

"But you never tell me anything about my mum and dad," Tilly went on. "How do I know what else you've been keeping from me? I'm not some little kid anymore; I can cope with the truth, even if it's something bad. How am I supposed to know who I really am if I don't know anything about my family?"

"We're your family, Tilly," Grandad said. "And we talk about your mum all the time."

"That's not true at all!" Tilly exploded. "You never talk about her. When I ask you about her you change the subject as soon as possible, and you mention her in passing, but you never tell me anything real about her."

"But what else do you want to know?" Grandad said.

"I want to know everything!" Tilly said, feeling angry tears threaten to fall. "I want to know what she was like when she was little, when she was my age, when she was pregnant. I want to know her favorite meal and her favorite film and her . . . her . . . her favorite type of cheese! I want to know what made her laugh and what made her cross and what made her excited. I want to know what it would have been like to have her help me with my homework; I want to know what it would be like to remember her reading to me; I want to know what she would say to me to make Grace stay friends with me; I want to know how she'd make sure Oskar didn't get bored of me either."

Tilly took a deep breath. "I just want to know what it would be like to know that she was always here, what it's like just having a normal mum."

Grandad looked stricken and half stood up as if to go to her, before sitting back down abruptly.

Grandma sniffed loudly and then steeled herself. "Tilly, I am sorry," she said. "I'm sorry that we haven't shared more of your mum with you. I'm sorry that we haven't been able to see outside our own sadness to realize we've left you with gaps. Let us try harder? I hope that being able to bookwander will help you feel a little closer to her, and all things considered I think that now is probably the time to—"

"Not now, Elsie," Grandad said. "It's too much."

"No," Grandma said gently. "Tilly can cope. I don't think we should keep it from her anymore."

"She left because of me, didn't she?" Tilly said, feeling sick. "I always knew it."

"No, that is the farthest thing from the truth," Grandma said firmly. "This is about her relationship with your father."

Tilly felt even sicker. "What did he do?" she asked.

"Tilly, when your mum finished university she stayed on in New York for a year. We thought everything was completely normal until she turned up on our doorstep, heavily pregnant. She wouldn't tell us much to start with; she just kept saying that it was incredibly important that you were born at home. We assumed she meant at Pages & Co., that she wanted to have you at home, with us, not in a different country. But, once you were born, and we were all so in love with you, she told us the truth."

Grandma reached her arms across the table and took Tilly's hands in hers.

"Matilda, we've told you that your mum had a special relationship with one particular book, *A Little Princess.* And that's the truth, but there's more to it. While she was bookwandering there, she fell in love with a fictional character, and later realized she was going to have a baby. Tilly, you share a dad with Sara. Your father is Captain Crewe."

25

More Than Neat Plot Devices

Tilly stared at Grandma.

"What? Captain Crewe? But . . . he's a character from a book. How is that possible?" Tilly paused. "Does that mean I'm not really real?" she whispered.

"No! Not at all," Grandma said, squeezing Tilly's hand. "You are absolutely as real as we are. You were born here; you're rooted in the real world. That's why your mum made sure to come home. She loved you so much that she left your dad, knowing that it would be impossible to be able to get back to him, to make sure you were safe. If she had stayed and had you in the novel, you would have been part of that story, and, if Bea had ever left the book, you would have just stopped existing once the text reverted. She gave up your dad for you, Tilly, so you could have a life and a future full of choice and freedom and all the messiness that comes with being a real person."

"Is that why she disappeared?" Tilly asked. "She wanted to get back to him?"

"No," Grandma said. "I know that in an ideal world she would have wanted nothing more than for the three of you to be together, but she knew in her heart that she would never have been able to find him. She could have gone back to Captain Crewe, of course, but he would never be the man she fell in love with. He wouldn't even remember her. He was always cursed to snap back to his written self as soon as she left that copy of the book; it's why bookwandering can never be a replacement for real life. I know that she visited afterward, but it could never be the same and she always came back home. She chose you, Tilly. It's why we know with such certainty that she didn't leave you."

"There's one more thing now you know the truth about your father, and it's important," Grandad said. "For now, it's vital that the Underlibrary does not find out who your father is. We hope they would be sensible about it, but there's no way of knowing how they would react. Enoch Chalk must not find out. He is a traditionalist and a hardliner: for him the rules are the most important thing and there is no space for personal feelings or irregular circumstances, and he is not the only one who thinks like that. Bookwanderers—for obvious reasons—are not supposed to fall in love with characters, and sadly there are some who would have it that you never should have been born. And, now you exist, we suspect that Chalk especially would prefer to find a way to return you to *A Little Princess* forever. I don't want to scare you, but you have to understand the risks. You must keep yourself safe. Chalk does not like rules being broken and he does not like anomalies."

"So, I'm an anomaly?" Tilly said.

"Well, yes, technically, you are, love," Grandad went on. "But we're all anomalies in one way or another—it's what makes being alive beautiful. We're more than neat plot devices: we're contradictory and confusing, and it's wonderful. There's nothing wrong with a few contradictions, and I think you might have to embrace them, as it would already seem that there are going to be some unpredictable side effects caused by your dad being fictional. The fact that you could see characters that your grandma and I were talking to should be impossible. The fact that Alice and Anne remembered you even after they'd journeyed back inside their books, again impossible. Go carefully while you're exploring bookwandering; now is not the time to explore too far. And, just as you should be wary of Chalk, you can trust Amelia within reason. There's no need to take the risk of telling her the whole truth, but, if you ever need to talk to someone who isn't us, find Amelia."

Tilly nodded but looked at her hands, still clasped in her grandma's, as though she might have changed or even vanished.

"So, what did happen to my mum?"

"We don't know, Tilly. But there's no reason to think it's anything to do with bookwandering, I promise you," Grandad said gently.

"Have you done one of those stamp things on her, to check?" Tilly asked.

"Yes, of course," Grandad said. "We've done everything we can to check it's not a bookwandering accident. The stamp showed no trace of her. You know everything we do about what happened; your mum popped into town for a coffee and never came back. Everything we've told you about your mum's disappearance is the truth: the police investigation, the lack of any evidence. That's all we know. It's a horrible, unhappy, fiercely real thing, which we have no reason to think is anything to do with the Underlibrary, or bookwandering, or your father."

"I'm going to go upstairs for a bit, I think," Tilly said after a pause. She needed a moment away from other people; there was too much information, too many secrets, too many concerned looks. Too much magic and excitement colliding with too much sadness and loss.

Upstairs, her mum's copy of *A Little Princess* was lying on Tilly's bedside table. It felt hot in her hands; it was no longer just an innocent story but a family archive. She opened it at the first page and with only a moment's hesitation read

her

way

in.

26

The Last Page

"Once on a dark winter's day, when the yellow fog hung so thick and heavy in the streets of London that the lamps were lighted and the shop windows blazed with gas as they do at night, an odd-looking little girl sat in a cab with her father, and was driven rather slowly through the big thoroughfares."

Tilly found herself with her feet in a freezing cold puddle at the mouth of an unlit, empty alleyway, not inside a cab, although she realized in hindsight that was probably for the best. It was bitterly cold, and at first sniff the air smelled of freshly baked bread, but there was something sour lurking underneath. The dirty water seeped through Tilly's sneakers as she pressed herself against a damp wall and waited for something to happen. Just as she was starting to worry that things had gone horribly wrong a black hansom cab rolled slowly past and Tilly caught a glimpse of a round pale face with large eyes staring out of the window.

Tilly ran to the end of the alleyway and poked her head round the corner to see that the cab had stopped outside a large brick building with

on a big brass plate on the front door.

A tall man wearing a thick gray overcoat stepped down from the cab and placed a shiny black top hat on his head. He moved with the elegance and confidence of someone whom the world had always rewarded simply for being alive. He reached back inside the cab and lifted down a small girl in a full coat, with dark hair cut into a blunt bob, and the two of them held hands as they walked up the steps to the door and rang the bell. Tilly could see them whispering and giggling nervously with each other as they waited, and as the door opened to an unsmiling woman in a maid's dress the girl pressed tightly into the man's side.

Tilly felt frozen to the spot, trying to drink in every detail of the man on the steps, wishing she was closer so she could see his face properly. The sight of his protective arm round Sara's shoulders filled her with a prickly feeling of envy, and she could almost feel the lack of his arm round herself, like a phantom limb. Even after they had gone inside, she found herself unable to move. Despite the cold and fog, she felt hot and flushed, and didn't know what to do next. She clutched her mum's copy of the book close to her chest and tried to think about what her mother would do, as the tiny glimpse of her father started to unravel her from inside.

"Be brave, be curious, be kind," she repeated to herself under her breath, as candlelight flared up in one of the front windows of the school and Tilly saw the dimly lit shapes of people moving around inside.

"Excuse me, miss, do you have any spare pennies?" a quiet cockney accent said.

Tilly looked down to see a girl who could only have been six or seven tugging at the edge of her jumper. Her face was dirty and her hair a tangled mess. She was quite obviously starving, and Tilly rummaged in the pockets of her jeans, finding twenty pence.

"I only have this, I'm afraid," Tilly said, holding out the coin. "I'm not even sure you'll be able to do anything with it, considering . . ."

The little girl turned it over in her hand.

"Are you sure I can have this, miss?" she said.

"Of course," Tilly said, wishing she had something far more useful or warm to give the little girl. The ragged girl bobbed a hasty curtsy and scurried across the road to a bakery lit up from within. Tilly shivered and kept her eyes on the school.

After half an hour or so, the front door opened again and Captain Crewe and Sara left. A tall woman dressed in black stood on the top step and waved them off, a broad smile on her face that dropped as soon as the cab door was closed again.

Tilly stared at the retreating cab before flicking forward in the book to find the next scene with the man her brain was still adjusting to thinking of as her father. The fog swirled in tight around her so she couldn't even see her hand stretched out in front of her. It buffeted her hair and she struggled to stay on her feet, but as fast as it had billowed it dissipated, and she found herself inside the school itself, in a decadently decorated room full of eerily lifelike dolls and clothes. Within seconds the door handle started to turn and Tilly spun round, looking for somewhere to hide, sliding herself behind the rich velvet curtains just as the door opened. The deep voice of Captain Crewe filled the space as he and Sara said goodbye to each other.

"Are you learning me by heart, little Sara?" Tilly heard her father say.

"No," a small but strong voice replied. "I know you by heart. You are inside my heart."

Tilly stood still behind the heavy curtains as she heard them hug each other fiercely, tears running silently down her cheeks as she cried for the father both she and Sara were about to lose. After she'd heard the click of the door closing, she slipped back out into the room, only to realize that Sara was still there, sitting cross-legged on the floor, staring into the distance.

"Hello," she said politely to Tilly, not seeming particularly surprised that a girl had just emerged from behind her curtains. "If you don't mind, I would quite like to be by myself at the moment, if you please. So, could you come back later, if you are coming to help me unpack?"

"I'm not a . . . I just . . ." Tilly had no idea how to explain herself so instead she left Sara sitting by herself and closed the door quietly behind her, nearly crashing into a skinny girl wearing a neat but very old dress with a dirty white apron over the top of it, with a mobcap on her frizzy brown hair.

"I'm so sorry, miss," she said, looking at the floor, and in doing so noticing Tilly's sneakers. She looked up in surprise, and her mouth dropped open as she took in all of Tilly.

"I don't mean to be rude, miss," she whispered, "but who are you? If you're not supposed to be here and Miss Minchin finds you . . . I hope I'm not being out of line, but you aren't dressed like any of the other girls, or anyone I've seen before. Are you from India, like Miss Crewe?"

"No, not India, but somewhere else that's rather far away,

I suppose. Somewhere I really should be getting back to. It was nice to meet you, Becky," Tilly said.

"How do you know my name?" Becky sounded surprised, but Tilly was already heading down the corridor, although she didn't know what to do next. She had no idea how she might find Captain Crewe now he had left the story, and she did not know what she would say to him even if she could find him.

She decided the most sensible thing to do would be to return to Pages & Co., make a plan, and then read herself back into the beginning when Captain Crewe and Sara first visit the school. She could go to those opening pages as many times as she wanted, like watching a favorite film over and over again.

She turned to the back of her mum's copy of *A Little Princess*, wondering if she should bring Oskar with her when she returned, and then stopped in horror as she realized that the last few pages were ripped and unreadable. The bottom corner of the last page was torn, as if caught in a bag, or just worn out from reading and folding and bending. Whatever had happened, it rendered the last few pages a mystery. Tilly slid her back down the wall into a corner, as she tried to get her ragged breathing under control. She stared at the book in her hands, chastising herself for not checking before she set off, especially so soon after Grandad had made it clear how careful she had to be. Hadn't she learned anything from *Treasure Island*?

Tilly decided there was nothing else for it but to read the last line that was there and hope for the best. She took some deep breaths, tried to block out the shrieking of girls playing downstairs, and read: "*Then she told him the story of the bun shop, and the fourpence she picked up out of the sloppy mud, and the child who . . .*"

Without warning everything suddenly went black, as though the whole world had been plunged into a power cut.

27

The Ordinances of Bookwandering

The blackness was so dense that it seemed almost like a physical object that Tilly could reach out and touch. She imagined it sneaking its way inside her nose and mouth and ears and she started to panic.

"Stop," she told herself sternly. "Be patient. Wait. Something usually happens at this point. Wait for the magic to kick in." She concentrated on trying to control the feeling of panic rising inside her and told herself that in just a moment fog would billow, or the walls would fold and slide, and her bedroom or the bookshop would materialize around her.

She scrunched up her eyes and stood completely still, waiting for the bookwandering magic to work. But, after what felt like an awfully long time in the inky blackness, Tilly was forced to come to terms with the fact that she definitely was not back at Pages & Co., and she did not seem to be in *A Little Princess* either.

She took stock of what she could sense. She was standing on something reassuringly solid and ground-like and she was warm. She could smell wood and paper and something sweet, but could not feel anything in her immediate arm span. She held her arms out in front of her and walked tentatively forward until she found something that felt comfortingly like a wall, not an infinite ether trapping her between stories.

"Okay, if this is a room, then there must be a door, or a window," Tilly muttered, trying to reassure herself. Eventually her fingertips brushed against what felt encouragingly like a door frame, and as she swished her hands around, she found a cold, round handle. She took a deep breath, turned and pulled it, and a door clicked open.

Tilly sagged in relief. Outside was not much better, but there was a muted gray light instead of soupy darkness and it was enough to be able to see a light switch right by the door, which Tilly turned on to reveal a very mundane, empty room. There was a small desk in one corner, with a wooden chair behind it, and a stack of notebooks on top. A dead plant was in one corner of the room, and there was a bin with just a rotten apple core inside it in another. Something about the smell and the feel of the place scratched at the back of Tilly's brain until it dawned on her where she was: the British Underlibrary.

She edged along the corridor—where most of the lights were off apart from the occasional door outline in gold—trying to get her bearings. She quietly followed the corridor round, hoping she would be able to find Amelia Whisper's office, and that Amelia would still be there, before Tilly had to knock on a door at random. They were all numbered, so she hoped that meant she was already in the right corridor, but as she looked for number forty-two she realized that the numbers didn't go in any recognizable pattern or order—and office one hundred and eleven was next to thirty-one, which was opposite six. It was no help at all and Tilly felt like she was back in Wonderland, until with a sigh of relief she saw door number forty-two with a soft glow of light leaking out from around it.

As Tilly went to knock she couldn't help but notice that the next door along, Chalk's office, was not lit up. She paused with her hand in the air, about to knock on Amelia's door, before pulling it back and putting her ear against Chalk's door instead. As she leaned against it the door clicked open and she tumbled noisily inside.

"Enoch?" she heard a muffled call from the office next door. "Everything okay?"

Tilly hurriedly but gently pushed the door closed and stayed as still as she could, pressing herself up against the wall of Chalk's office. She heard Amelia push her chair back and open her door, and Tilly held her breath, but a second later she heard Amelia retreating into her own office.

Faced with Chalk's empty office, Tilly realized she was acting primarily on instinct, rather than hard-and-fast clues, but she could not shake the uneasy feeling that there was more to

Chalk than Grandma and Grandad had let on, or maybe more than they knew. His excuses for talking to her in *Anne of Green Gables*, or being in *Alice in Wonderland*, were setting off alarm bells and raising red flags, and Tilly had read enough books to know not to ignore them.

She switched on the desk light, which cast a dim glow and eerie shadows round the office. The room was pristine, with barely anything on the desk apart from a computer that was turned off, and a shallow wire tray with a few sheets of paper in it. Tilly flicked through them, and saw that they were all covered in lists of bookshops printed in tiny type. Some of them were crossed out with angry red lines, and some were marked with arrows or stars.

There were no photos or knickknacks, no garish "Best Librarian" mugs, no sign of personality anywhere. The only decoration was a large poster pinned to the back of the door titled "The Ordinances of Bookwandering." As she looked closer she realized it was handwritten. As her eyes scanned the list, she felt increasingly nervous. These rules were devoid of the sense of adventure or wonder that seemed to fill Amelia or Seb when they talked about bookwandering.

"One: Travel within a Source Edition without prior permission, training, or qualifications is strictly prohibited," Tilly read. *"Two: Entry to the Source Library, as above. Three: All bookwanderers should be registered immediately after abilities manifest themselves, otherwise traveling will be classed as willfully illicit. Four: No*

bookwanderer is permitted within five pages of the end of a novel unless trained in Endpapers Travel."

The rules went on and on, all seeming to ban something or other. Tilly shuddered and moved over to the shelves of fat ledgers that lined the room. She noticed they were embossed in small gold letters with the dates they covered and pulled one down at random. She saw rows and rows of names and bookshops and libraries, written in handwriting that changed every few years. Tilly ran her fingertips down the thick paper, down the records of so many different people and their stories, and wondered what adventures they had had. She liked knowing that her mum was in one of the ledgers somewhere, and that Grandma and Grandad must be in one too. Generations of bookwanderers all listed together in nearly identical emerald-green ledgers. She wondered if anyone other than Chalk ever looked at them.

As she put back the ledger she realized the office was not as entirely lacking in personality as she had first thought. At the back, tucked away in a corner, was a bookcase of the sort of books you might expect to find in a librarian's office—novels, children's books, classics, a large blue book of fairy tales. A colorful, messy mix of books. It made Tilly wonder if they'd judged Chalk too harshly after all; could anyone with a full set of Harry Potter novels be that bad? He even had a copy of *A Little Princess*, and Tilly felt her heart thaw an extra degree toward him.

Tilly forgot where she was for a moment and pulled down

his copy; it was a different edition from her mum's, which was tucked under her arm, or any she'd seen before at the bookshop. The cover was a simple black matte one with the title and the author's name in gold writing. She flicked through the first few chapters, unable to resist reading the description of her father again, but she was instantly distracted by the scene in which Captain Crewe and Sara first leave the school, which was not quite how she remembered it. She was sure she hadn't seen their cab swerve in the road to avoid hitting someone, but she was also learning that once you were inside a book anything was possible. But then she found another passage that she was sure was different in her mum's copy.

She read it out loud under her breath to herself.

"*She went into the shop. It was warm and smelled deliciously. A young woman, wrapped in a warm cloak, stood at the counter, absentmindedly playing with her necklace as she waited for the baker to finish setting out the piping hot buns.*

'Good morning, miss. How are the children doing in this cold weather?'

'Quite well, thank you, Nancy. They're all very excited about Christmas.'

The baker smiled warmly. 'What can I get you then? Anything for the little ones?'

'A loaf of bread, and some of those tiny almond cakes, please? There are several sweet teeth back at the house.'

The goods were wrapped up neatly in waxed paper and the

woman left the bakery in a gust of cold air as the door closed. The woman behind the counter noticed Sara, shivering in her thin dress.

'If you please,' said Sara, 'have you lost fourpence—a silver fourpence?'"

Tilly slid the book back onto the shelf and put her own on Chalk's desk to check, confused by the differences. Perhaps she was misremembering the scene. Was her mum's copy special somehow? But, before she could turn up the right page in her book to check, the door handle started to turn. She froze; there was nowhere to hide and all she had time to do was shove her mum's copy of the book into her pinafore dress, thankful it had large pockets, before the door was flung open to reveal Enoch Chalk silhouetted in the hazy gray light, looking furious.

"Come here, girl," he snarled. "I knew there was something strange about you the moment I first saw you."

Tilly backed into the corner. "I'm s-sorry, Mr. Chalk," she stammered. "I got lost and I couldn't work out how to get home and your door was open and I—"

"Enough," he interrupted. "No excuses. How did you get here, Miss Pages?"

"Like I said, I was lost in the library and your door was—"

"No," he said, tense with anger. "We will get to why you are in my office in good time. I want to know how you have come to be in the Underlibrary past closing hours and by yourself?" He spun round. "Is your grandfather here too?"

"No! No. I didn't mean to come here," Tilly protested. "I

promise. It was an accident. I was trying to get out of a book, but the page was torn and—"

"What on earth is going on here?"

Tilly was faint with relief when she saw Amelia Whisper join Chalk at the door. "I thought you had gone home, Enoch. Why are you out in the corridor bellowing . . . ?" Amelia tailed off as she caught sight of Tilly. "Matilda? What on earth are you doing back here?"

28

Stories Are for Reading

"Okay, let's go and sit down in my office," Amelia said, shepherding Tilly out. Chalk went to follow, but Amelia put her hand in his way. "I think I just need a moment to chat with Tilly by myself first, Enoch, if you would excuse us."

"She broke into my office!" Chalk spluttered in indignation.

"I know, I know, but, as you said yourself, we need to understand why she is in the library at all before we get to that. Maybe you could go and find us some cups of tea?"

"I am not a tea lady, Ms. Whisper," Chalk said coldly.

"Well, perhaps you could go and find us one then, Enoch. Or, indeed, a tea man."

Amelia guided Tilly into her office with a gentle hand on her back as Chalk stalked off down the corridor.

"I actually have a kettle in my office," Amelia said with a smile, "but I thought we should have a chance to talk by ourselves.

Tilly, it's really important that you tell me the truth at this point, okay?" Tilly nodded. "How did you get back into the library this evening? Did you hide somewhere? Is Oskar here too?"

"No, we went back home, all three of us, I promise," Tilly said.

"Okay, so your grandparents don't know you're here?" Amelia asked.

Tilly shook her head.

"Well, first things first: we need to tell them that you're safe with me and they can come and get you." She picked up the phone on her desk. "Hello, Archie? This is Amelia. We've got Tilly here. She's completely safe and is with me. We . . . Yes, yes, I know . . . We can talk about this later, but the most important thing is for you to come and get her. Yes . . . Yes . . . No. See you soon then." She put the phone down and turned to Tilly. "They're on their way. And I'm guessing that your grandad must have filled you in a bit more about everything after you left this afternoon?"

"A bit," Tilly said vaguely, remembering what Grandma and Grandad had told her about keeping the details about her father a secret.

"It must have been difficult to hear about everything that happened eleven years ago. No one thought your grandparents did anything wrong really, but—"

"What?" Tilly interrupted. "Why would anyone think my grandparents had done anything wrong?"

"Well, of course they didn't take the accusations seriously— but because Archie was your mum's father I'm sure you can imagine that there had to be a full investigation into how Bea got into the Source Library. Thankfully the Archivists weren't involved."

Amelia stopped, registering the look of confusion on Tilly's face. "You look surprised—I . . . I thought you said your grandparents told you about this?"

"I thought you meant—" Tilly stopped abruptly. "They didn't say anything about the Source Library. They just told me more about my mum being a bookwanderer too," she finished lamely.

Amelia looked at her intently.

"So, what did my mum do?" Tilly pushed.

"It's not really my story to tell, Tilly, but the headline is that she stole your grandad's key to the Source Library because she was trying to access one of the books to change it permanently, and I'm sure you understand how troubling that is. But really this is something you should talk to your grandparents about properly. We both saw this morning that your grandad is obviously very particular about the way he wants to tell you these sorts of things.

"In the meantime we need to get back to the matter at hand, Tilly. Don't worry; you're not in trouble. It's just that only very senior bookwanderers have clearance to access the library via any route other than the King's Library elevator, so we need to understand how you got here."

"I wanted to practice bookwandering," Tilly explained.

"So I read myself into a book, and it worked completely fine, but when I tried to get out I saw that the final page was torn, so I just read the last bit that was there, and then everything went black and I ended up in an empty room down the corridor from here. I wasn't trying to get here, I promise. I didn't even know where I was to start with. And then, when I realized, I came to try to find you, or one of the other librarians, so I could get home."

"Via Mr. Chalk's office?" Amelia quirked an eyebrow. "But we'll come back to that. Can I ask which book it was you traveled into? Do you have it with you still?"

Tilly paused before handing over her mum's old copy of *A Little Princess*.

"Ah," she said gently, looking carefully at Tilly. "Your mother's favorite."

"Yes . . ." Tilly said, eyeing her warily. "How do you know?"

"Well, Tilly, it's no secret that your mum and I were good friends a long time ago. It's why I wanted to speak to you on your own first, without Mr. Chalk here. We met in New York. We worked at the same bookshop there. I haven't seen her since she went back home, pregnant with you. Until your grandad brought you to the library this morning, you didn't exist according to the bookwandering community. After your grandad resigned as Librarian, he and Elsie went off the radar. Everyone assumed that they just wanted a quiet life away from all of the bookwandering politics, and to try to take care of Bea a bit."

"Why does Mr. Chalk seem so angry all the time?" Tilly asked.

"Well, Enoch is very good at his job, in many ways—he has a bit of a sixth sense for anything going awry—but he has a different perspective on bookwandering. He is fond of rules and I'm afraid your mum broke most of those rules. He thinks we should be far stricter about bookwandering: how we monitor it, how we regulate it, if there should be an age restriction, whether we should allow anyone to do it who demonstrates a natural ability. He's written seemingly endless reports questioning what books and stories are really for."

"But stories are for reading," Tilly said. "Why do they have to be for something anyway? Can't they just be?"

"I am rather inclined to agree with you, Tilly, as are your grandparents, but that doesn't mean everyone else is. With regard to Enoch I'm not yet sure that we can explain your appearance here in the Underlibrary. Somehow you were pulled back to the library and were able to get past the barriers we have to protect this place. I think we would be ill-advised to share this ability widely. In fact, I think the best plan is for me to handle it, and to try to avoid you crossing paths with Enoch again on this visit. Although I need to ask you, Tilly, why you were in his office?"

Tilly flushed. "I'm sorry, I know I shouldn't have been. I saw his door and I just didn't think. I was curious."

"We don't keep the offices locked here, Tilly, because the library is so well protected from the outside world, but that doesn't mean that you should enter people's private spaces without their permission. I think you probably understand this. I will pass your apologies on to Mr. Chalk."

Tilly nodded and at that moment Amelia's phone rang. She listened silently and then put the phone back in its cradle.

"Okay, your grandparents are on their way. They'll be here in about fifteen minutes. Do you have any more questions?"

"Can I ask you about Grandma?" Tilly said. "I know Grandad was the Librarian when he worked here, but Grandma said she worked here too before everything with my mum happened—what did she do?"

"Ah, good question. Your grandma was our Cartographer. She worked in the Map Room where . . . Actually, would you like to see it quickly while we wait?"

Tilly nodded.

They walked back through the library hall, which was dimly lit. A handful of librarians were working at desks and another was dozing behind the main desk. Amelia's footsteps startled the sleeper awake and she sat up straighter, wiping her mouth self-consciously with her cardigan sleeve. Tilly and Amelia went back out the other end, toward the lift, and stopped at one of the rooms Tilly had walked past with Grandad and Oskar earlier that day.

29

Book Magic Is the Only Sort We Have

The room was far bigger than any of the offices Tilly had seen so far and was hexagonal in shape. The floor was painted the same deep turquoise as the ceiling of the main hall, but the six walls and the ceiling were all lined with beautiful, intricate maps pricked with constellations of tiny lights in different colors.

"This is the Map Room," Amelia said, smiling.

Tilly looked around in wonder. "What's it for?"

"This is what your grandma looked after. These lights are all bookshops across the whole world. The white lights are bookshops where there are known bookwanderers, the blue lights are national Underlibraries, the yellow lights are shops where we have no bookwanderers to our knowledge, and the scarlet lights are those where there used to be bookwanderers, but aren't anymore. And the green lights are libraries. We have to keep track because, as you know, bookshops and libraries are key to bookwandering," Amelia said. "And we must treasure the bookshops and libraries we have left."

"How do you keep track of them all? Is that magic too?" Tilly asked.

"I'm afraid not," Amelia said. "It's old-fashioned emails and letters and phone calls and admin; book magic is the only sort we have at our disposal. The current Cartographer, Aria, is in charge of our relationships with all the other Underlibraries around the world, and she keeps abreast of what's going on: how many bookwanderers there are in different countries, patterns, agreed international rules, that sort of thing. Go on, take a closer look; here's the UK," Amelia said, pointing at a map centered on one wall.

Tilly traced her finger down the map until she found London: a comforting cluster of glowing lights. Many were white, but there was also a smattering of gold and scarlet. A small, glowing blue beacon identified the Underlibrary itself. Next to every light was a tiny scrawl of writing naming each shop. On the outskirts of the galaxy of London bookshops was one marked "*Pages & Co.*" in looping handwriting. It shone bright white, and Tilly's heart glowed in tandem with the pinprick of light.

"Is the bookshop you worked in with my mum on here?" she asked.

Amelia took her over to the opposite wall, which was nearly all taken up with North America, and found a label that said

"*Bennet & Eyre*" among the cluster of New York lights. She touched the words gently. "It was a pretty special place—owned by a brother and sister. One day, when we have more time, I'll tell you all about that shop—but for now we should probably go and check if your grandparents have arrived. This room is not a secret; you can visit it whenever you're here. You should get your grandma to bring you back and tell you more about it."

Outside the Map Room, Amelia paused, and handed Tilly her mum's copy of *A Little Princess*.

"It should go without saying, but please do not try to travel inside your mother's copy of *A Little Princess* again; it's clearly unstable without its final lines. I think we might need to look at this again at some point, and work out why you were brought here, but as long as I can trust you not to wander inside this copy you can keep hold of it for now. I know it belonged to your mum and will mean a lot to you." She looked intently at Tilly, who nodded her agreement but silently thought that she needed to have a much closer look and work out why this book was different before she let anyone else examine it.

They walked down the dim corridor into the main hall, back past the sleepy librarian. Amelia led Tilly through an unassuming door to what looked like a fire exit.

"Is this another magical lift?" Tilly asked, suddenly realizing quite how exhausted she was after all that had happened that day.

"No, this one's just a fire exit," Amelia said. "We do try to comply with up-to-date fire and safety regulations, even though no one knows we're here. Good faith, et cetera—we are librarians after all."

Tilly nodded as if she knew what Amelia meant and then the door swung open and a burst of bracing October night air knocked into her. She was immediately wrapped up in a hug from both her grandparents.

"Thank you, Amelia," Grandma said, holding Amelia's arm tightly. "Do we know what happened? We thought she might have headed there; we should have thought in advance . . ." She tailed off, realizing she'd said more than she had intended.

"Don't worry, Elsie; I don't think it's anything to cause concern," Amelia said. She paused. "I think that Tilly may have tumbled out here because of what I'd call a particularly strong connection to the Underlibrary, so when something went wrong she was pulled back here as a sort of protective measure. I wonder if Tilly's bookwandering may have some unusual side effects . . ."

"Why would you say that?" Grandma asked slowly.

"Just a hunch," Amelia said, looking Grandma directly in the eyes. Neither of them said anything more.

"So what went wrong?" Grandad asked.

"The last page of my book had been torn," Tilly said.

"I genuinely don't think we have any cause for concern," Amelia said firmly. "Tilly knows not to travel into that book again, and this is a good lesson in the importance of following the bookwandering rules. Maybe when Tilly's found her feet a bit more with bookwandering, and had a little time to digest everything she's learned today, we can revisit this, but no reason to worry for now. Much more important to get her home. But maybe watch some TV tonight instead of reading a book?" She smiled as she shook Grandad's hand and gave Grandma a warm hug.

Tilly climbed into the back of the waiting taxi that had brought Grandma and Grandad to the Underlibrary, and she was asleep long before they got back to Pages & Co.

30

Fairy Tales

The next morning Grandma woke Tilly up with a glass of orange juice and a plate of peanut butter on toast.

"Morning, sweetheart," she said. "How are you feeling? You've had a lot to think about—you know you can come and chat with me or Grandad anytime, if you want, and we'll be completely honest with you about bookwandering, or your mum and dad—as much as we know."

Tilly gave her a bit of a wobbly smile.

"Or Jack and I were going to do some party planning, if you wanted to join in with that for a bit? Maybe you could see if Oskar wants to come round and help too?"

Tilly nodded more confidently and took a big crunch of toast. A morning of day-to-day bookshop business was exactly what she wanted to give her time to think through everything that had happened yesterday—but first she had research to do. After finishing her breakfast, knowing she'd regret eating her toast in bed later, she picked up the ripped copy of *A Little Princess* and flicked back to the scene in the bakery. She was relieved to find she hadn't been imagining things—the story was undeniably, if unremarkably, different.

"There must be a reason my mum kept this one," Tilly said to herself, tucking it under her arm to go and compare it to the bookshop copies.

She went downstairs, through a warm but empty kitchen, and into the shop. Jack and Grandma were clustered round one of the café tables, laughing and making notes.

"I'm going to go and find Oskar!" Tilly called over as she made her way out onto the high street, which was littered with autumn leaves. But Crumbs was locked up and all the lights were off. Tilly pressed her face against the glass, but there was quite obviously no one there, and there was no note pinned to the door, or any kind of explanation. She pulled her phone out and sent Oskar a text.

`crumbs is closed? are you okay? Tilly x`

A few minutes later she had a reply.

my mamie is poorly :(mum closed shop to sort plans at home. oskar

`what's going on? t x`

mum might have to go to paris to help. or emilie might come back here for a bit. o

are you going to france too? t x

not sure. maybe. not today tho. waiting for more news.

do you want to come to the shop and help with the party? we can meet you at bus stop if your mum's worried?

will ask

And then, after a few minutes:

k, coming now. mum says thanks. she will call shop and speak to elsie or archie. no. 81?

no. 81, get off at beech court stop. see you soon. we have fresh doughnuts!!!!
t x

Tilly dashed back into the shop.

"Oskar's French grandmother isn't very well," she shouted over to Grandma. "Crumbs is closed—he's going to get the bus over from his flat, if that's okay? Mary's going to call you." And just as she said it the phone started ringing.

"Yes, of course, Mary. Yes, don't worry . . . We'll be there at the bus stop to meet him, I promise . . . Yes, Tilly has his phone number . . . No problem, as long as you need . . . Tell us if there's anything else we can do at all . . . Yes, speak soon . . ."

About half an hour later Tilly got a text from Oskar that he was nearly there and Jack went with her to wait at the bus stop round the corner. An exhausted-looking Oskar arrived a few minutes later. They exchanged glances that had to replace words that couldn't be said in front of Jack.

"All right, mate?" Jack said. "Sorry to hear your *mamie* is poorly. Do you want to talk about it or just get on as usual?"

"Get on as usual," Oskar said firmly. "I do *not* want anyone making a fuss."

"Sure thing," Jack said. "There's heaps to do around here for the party. Plenty to keep you occupied for hours! Elsie'll have you cutting out decorations all day, if you're not careful."

Grandma waved them over to her as they arrived back at the shop. Oskar stared at all the pieces of paper littering the table. Bad sketches, lists of people and ideas, lots of empty coffee mugs.

"Right, team," Grandma said. "On today's agenda: decorations, RSVP list, confirming food and drink."

"Isn't that everything?" Tilly asked, and Grandma laughed.

"Not even close, my darling. The party is tomorrow night

after all. Now, how do we feel about the decorations? Something to do with playing cards, I suppose?"

"Well, I was thinking I could do something along those lines in the window," Jack said. "Maybe try to copy one of the illustrations from the book? I'm not sure what would work best."

"Oskar's good at art," Tilly volunteered.

"Uh, no I'm not," he said.

"Yes you are. I saw you drawing the other day."

"Just because I like doing it doesn't mean I'm any good at it," Oskar said.

"Well, I bet you are," Tilly said.

"Why don't you have a doodle, see if you can come up with anything?" Grandma said encouragingly, pushing a pen and some blank paper toward Oskar. "We're not expecting you to be Picasso, don't worry. All ideas are useful. Look at what a state we're in!" Oskar looked unconvinced, but shielded the paper with his arm and started scratching.

After an hour of companionable silence, Jack went to refill the teapot, juice glasses, and the plate that had only a scattering of crumbs left on it. Oskar had gradually forgotten to keep his arm over his paper and now had several sheets laid out in front of him covered in colorful flowers and vines as well as sketches of impossibly high cream cakes. Interspersed with party ideas were doodles of pirate ships and treasure maps.

"Have you always enjoyed art, Oskar?" Grandma asked.

"Uh-huh." Oskar nodded as he drew. "Actually it was my *mamie* who first encouraged me. I used to always be scrawling on bits of paper, and she was a book illustrator when she was younger and helped me learn a bit more about, you know, actually making things look like real things."

"Ah, Oskar, I knew there had to be some literary lineage somewhere!" Grandma said in delight.

"Literary what?" he said.

"Lineage . . . It means your ancestors, your family, the people you're descended from. No wonder you were so attuned to bookwandering if your grandmother was an artist—what sort of thing did she illustrate, do you know?"

"All sorts, I think, although she always says the thing she was most proud of was this huge version of a book of fairy tales—she has some of her artwork from it up in her apartment in Paris."

"How wonderful," Grandma said. "We'll have to ask your mum which edition it is and see if we can track it down; I'd love to see her work. We should send her some of your drawings, Oskar; I'm sure it would make her happy to see them."

Oskar flushed and nodded, a small smile on his face.

"The thing is about bookwandering—" Grandma started, but stopped abruptly as Jack came back with a tray. Tilly and Oskar exchanged a look and went back to their paper.

"All still being very studious, I see," Jack said, setting

down a plate of scones with cream and jam. "I'm very impressed indeed. Oskar, you're clearly a good influence; it normally takes Elsie and Tilly forever to get anything done."

Grandma grinned at him affectionately as he sat back down and started working on the shopping list. As Oskar returned back to his drawings and Grandma looked back at the guest list, Tilly kicked her heels together, not sure how she was supposed to be helping.

"Why don't I go and get some copies of *Alice in Wonderland* maybe?" she suggested. "For inspiration."

"Ah, good idea, Tilly, yes, of course. But, um, don't stray too far, yes?" Grandma looked intently at her, and she nodded her understanding.

Once she arrived in the children's section, instead of heading for the C shelf to find Carroll, Lewis, Tilly went to the shelf above for Burnett, Frances Hodgson, and pulled down a few different copies of *A Little Princess*. She settled down to compare the books herself. She found the bakery scene in three different editions—and they were all the same as one another, but also the same as her mother's copy. Tilly felt a cold, leaden feeling settle in her stomach. She had been so sure she was going to find some clues to her parents' love story, and yet her mum's copy seemed to be entirely normal. She checked the whole opening, in which her father appeared, against all the books and had to accept they were word for word the same. Which meant, she realized with a jolt, that it was Chalk's copy that was different.

As she sat with the pile of books next to her a familiar voice said, "Why, hello again," and Alice settled down next to her in a rustle of petticoats.

"You look most perturbed," she said. "Do you want to escape for a bit with me?" She held out her hand to Tilly, who shuffled away.

"I've got to stay here and help," Tilly said firmly. "Plus, yesterday, I tried to go inside a book and everything went wrong." Tilly found herself distinctly wobbly about the idea of bookwandering after everything that had happened the day before, not to mention desperate for some time to herself to think about what she'd learned.

"Boring!" Alice said. "Firstly, no one will notice you've gone, and secondly you'll be with me so it's fine. Do you want to come and see the most beautiful garden?"

"Maybe you could stay here and talk instead? Or help?" Tilly said hopefully.

"What are you doing?" said Alice.

"We're getting ready for the party," Tilly said.

"Oh, how marvelous," Alice said, clapping her hands together in delight. "I love parties. Will you have games?"

"Um, maybe," Tilly said. "Although it's more of a chatting sort of party."

"That doesn't sound like a party to me, and I know the most wonderful game—it's called a caucus race."

"And how do you play that?" Tilly asked. "Isn't it kind of chaotic?"

Alice paused. "The best way to explain it is to do it, really."

"Well, you'll have to try, because I'm not coming with you," Tilly said.

"Fine," Alice huffed. "Well, you need a racetrack, which should be a circle sort of shape, but it doesn't really matter so much, and then everyone starts running until the race is finished."

"But how do you know when it has finished?" Tilly asked.

"I'm not quite sure, to be honest. The first time I saw it I was confused, I admit. Everyone got prizes, so I suppose everyone won."

"It doesn't sound like it makes much sense, and I don't think we could have a race in the shop anyway."

Alice sighed. "No, you're probably right. Sometimes being sensible is ever so dull, don't you find?"

"I suppose," Tilly said, "although sometimes being sensible is, well, the sensible thing to do."

"How contrary you sound," Alice replied. She paused. "I really do think you should come with me to the garden, you know; it's ever so beautiful."

"I can't. I promised Grandma I'd stay here. Maybe we could go after the party?" Tilly suggested.

"I would like to go now actually," Alice said. "I've not had a friend like you before and I want you to come with me." She leaned over and tried to grab Tilly's hand.

"No!" Tilly said, snatching her hand away, but Alice managed to get hold of her little finger and the shop began to melt away just as Tilly pulled her hand back.

"Bother," she heard Alice say as she faded away.

31

Curiosity Creates the Very Best Adventures

Tilly was in a garden, but Alice was not. The garden was beautiful, though, Alice had been right about that. There were red roses growing everywhere, with ornate fountains dotted around bright flower beds. Tilly absentmindedly touched a rose and was alarmed to see that her fingers came away red. She thought she had pricked her finger until she realized that it was paint and that the roses were white underneath a messy layer of red paint. *Of course*, she thought, *I'm in the Queen of Hearts's garden*, and she started looking for Alice with more urgency. A small wooden door in a tree was suddenly flung open and Tilly nearly fell over as a giant version of Alice's face appeared at the doorway.

"What are you doing in there? And why are you so big?" Tilly whispered.

"Oh bother," Alice said. "I've ended up on the wrong side again. Hang on."

"No!" Tilly shouted after her. "I'll come through to you! I'm small enough to get through the door and I don't fancy running into the Queen of Hearts by myself, not with her habit of chopping people's heads off."

It was a bit of a squeeze to get through the door in the tree, but when Tilly did she realized that she only came up to Alice's knee.

Alice picked her up carefully and took her over to a huge three-legged table made of glass and placed her on top. There was a bottle with a paper label marked "DRINK ME" and a tiny golden key, and Tilly felt as though she was experiencing déjà vu. Alice was crouched down on the floor, looking for something.

"Aha, here it is," she said triumphantly, setting down a cake next to the bottle. The cake was marked EAT ME in raisins. "Now, if I could just remember which way round they are . . ."

"I think maybe the cake is for growing, and the drink for shrinking," Tilly said, "seeing as how the cake was on the floor and the bottle is up here."

"Now, you say that, but things here can be rather topsy-turvy, so perhaps the opposite is true," Alice said, reaching for the bottle.

"No, no, no!" Tilly shouted. "I definitely think you should just try a crumb of the cake first. And—Stop, Alice! Wait! You need to put me on the floor first, with the bottle, so we have all the options available."

Alice stared at her. "You're ever so logical," she said in a pitying voice. "No wonder you don't fit in here."

"Since when was being logical a bad thing?" Tilly said accusingly. "It means you don't get stuck at the wrong size constantly."

"Now, I know you must have a good imagination, otherwise you couldn't be here, but it's hardly on display. Curiosity creates the very best adventures in my experience. That's what your mother used to say, isn't it?"

"Yes. Be brave, be curious, be kind," Tilly said.

"Well, exactly. She sounds like she knew what she was talking about." And with that Alice placed Tilly down on the floor alongside the bottle and popped the whole cake into her mouth in one go. Within seconds she had shrunk to the same size as Tilly.

"You'd better have that key," Tilly said. Alice opened her palm to reveal it shining in her hand.

Alice grinned triumphantly. "Shall we?"

They walked back to the tiny door, which Alice made a great song and dance about opening with a dramatic flourish, and they were back in the beautiful garden with its roses dripping with paint.

Alice touched one gingerly and her fingertips came away red.

"I wonder why they have been painted," she said. "They already looked so beautiful."

"It's because it's the Queen of Hearts's garden," Tilly said. "You must know that; it's your story."

"It's the queen's garden?" Alice said in horror. "I've heard the most monstrous things about her. We must make sure she doesn't spot us."

"What? How do you—"

But Tilly was interrupted by three gardeners, all dressed as playing cards, manically dabbing at roses that had not yet been painted.

"Look out now, Five! Don't go splashing paint over me like that!"

"I couldn't help it," said the Five of Spades. "Seven jogged my elbow!"

"That's right, Five!" grumbled the third gardener. "Always lay the blame on others."

The arguing went on for ages until Seven threw its paintbrush down, splattering bursts of red paint all over the grass and the other gardeners. It turned away from them, crossing its arms in a sulk, and laid eyes on Tilly and Alice, watching them with mouth open.

"Would you tell me, please," asked Alice, "why you are painting those roses?"

"Why, the fact is, you see, Miss," said the Two of Spades, "this here ought to have been a *red* rose-tree and we put a white one in by mistake, and if the Queen was to find it out, we should all have our heads cut off, you know. So you see, Miss, we're doing our best, afore she comes, to—"

But it was too late, and the gardeners flung themselves to the ground as Tilly heard a great racket coming toward them.

"Let's go," Tilly hissed, pulling at Alice's hand, and they darted behind a bush just before the royal parade came round the corner. Tilly gasped as she saw a procession of playing cards followed by a great gaggle of people, a white rabbit wearing a waistcoat and pocket watch, and then the King and Queen of Hearts themselves. They were both quite square-looking and dressed in incredibly ornate robes, like the Tudor kings and queens from Tilly's history books at school. The king had some very elaborate facial hair, with a beard that ended in an extravagant curl on his chin. The queen had a gravity-defying hairstyle and was clutching a large gilt hand mirror shaped like a heart.

"Please can we go back to Pages & Co.?" Tilly said, not liking the look of the queen at all.

"Hang on, hang on," Alice said. "I want to watch. I don't mind if you don't stay, though."

"But how do I get back without you?" Tilly said desperately as the queen stalked ever closer to them.

"I don't think you can, my darling," said a new voice, and Tilly spun round to see a wide grin floating in the air right next to her ear.

32

You Can Walk Off the End of Any Story

The smile hovered and flickered as it grinned at Tilly. She nudged Alice, who huffed at being torn away from watching the chaotic croquet game that was now going on—were those flamingos?—and turned.

"What is it? I've already told you I don't want to take you back yet."

Tilly pointed at the smile. "Is that—" she started.

"Why, it's only the Cheshire Cat," Alice interrupted, and went back to watching the croquet—they were definitely flamingos. And at that the whole cat materialized: orange, stripy, and purring.

The cat noticed Tilly staring at it.

"Never heard a talking cat before?" it asked, and Tilly started. She knew it could talk from reading the book, but it was still surprising to hear a large cat say something in English.

"I haven't, actually," Tilly said. "But I met a talking dormouse, and a hare, the other day."

"Ah excellent," the cat replied. "You're obviously familiar with Wonderland and its inhabitants. How delightful to meet a fan." It curled its tail elegantly in Tilly's direction.

"How do you know you're in a story when no one else does?" Tilly said, looking sideways at Alice. "I haven't been able to get any straight answers out of anyone about this."

"You're not likely to get any straight answers from me either, I'm afraid." The cat grinned. "Although you're welcome to ask."

"I just don't understand what's real, and what's imagination," Tilly said.

"I find most things are a mixture of the two. And reality is overrated—she's an unpredictable mistress." The cat smiled again. "She shifts and slides and never behaves quite as you might like or expect. She's a tricksy friend to have. Not to mention that she's even more difficult in Wonderland."

"What do you mean?" Tilly asked.

"Well, is Wonderland really real at all? Is Wonderland more real than where Alice has come from, or where you have come from? You're both visitors to the land, and who's to say which or where or who has the greatest claim on reality?" the cat said.

"But this must be some sort of real; we're here right now," Tilly said, grabbing at a nearby rose bush, her head starting to spin.

"Are the things in your imagination less real than the things in front of you? Is this rose more real than you? Do the books you've read mean less to you because they haven't really happened to you? Do daydreams at midday or nightdreams at midnight mean nothing?"

"So am I really here?"

"Why, of course you are really here." The cat flashed its teeth mischievously. "But who's to say exactly where here really is, and who's to say where you're going. You might walk right off the end of Wonderland."

"I can walk off the end of Wonderland?" Tilly asked.

"You can walk off the end of any story," the cat said. "But remember to mind the gap. And don't tell them I told you."

"Don't tell who?" Tilly asked, even more confused.

"The secret keepers, the gate watchers, the border guards, the door lockers," the cat said languidly.

Tilly huffed. "You're no help at all."

The Cheshire Cat just grinned once more, before turning its attention to Alice.

"How are you getting on, dear Alice?" it asked. Alice started relaying how unjust the croquet game was in great detail.

"I don't think they play at all fairly," Alice complained. "And they all quarrel so dreadfully one can't hear oneself speak—and there don't seem to be any rules in particular; at least, if there are, nobody attends to them—and you've no idea how confusing it is all the equipment being alive . . ."

The cat good-naturedly rolled its eyes at Tilly as Alice went on at length.

"How do you like the queen?" it asked.

"Not at all!" exclaimed Alice. "She's so extremely . . ."

Alice paused as she realized that the game had ground to a halt and everyone involved was now staring in their direction. The queen held out a hand, which the king rapidly took hold of, and they strutted in Alice and Tilly's direction. As they approached them Alice kicked Tilly into a curtsy, but the king was more interested in the cat's floating head.

"Who *are* you talking to?" he said.

"A friend," Alice said as the cat shimmered in and out of existence, just to disconcert the king.

"I don't like the look of it at all," the king said a little rudely. "However, it may kiss my hand, if it likes."

"I'd really rather not," the cat said, and casually licked its sharp front teeth.

"Don't be impertinent," huffed the king. "My dear, my dear," he said to the queen. "Look at this strange creature I have discovered."

The queen peered at the cat. "Off with his head!" she shrieked. And, at that, everything descended once more into chaos, everyone arguing with everyone else, the queen calling for the executioner, and flamingos running amok. Amid the madness the cat winked at Tilly and dissolved away, so by the time an executioner had been found and shoved to the front by the queen there was no evidence it had ever been there at all.

"Shall we follow suit?" Alice asked, holding out her hand to Tilly, who grasped it firmly.

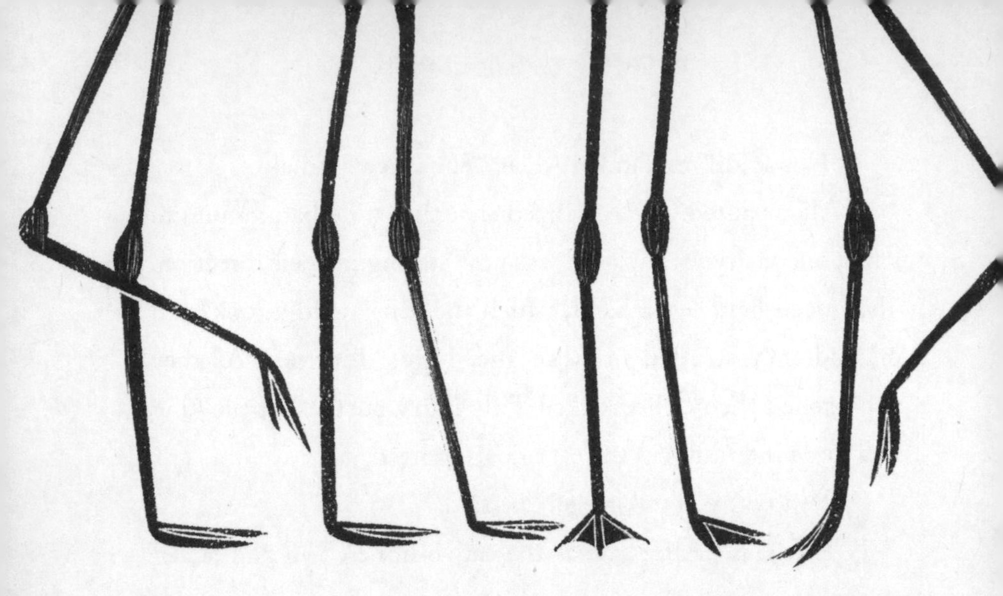

"Goodness," Alice said beside her, as Pages & Co. rebuilt itself around them, "it would have been quite the disaster to have our heads chopped off by the Queen of Hearts, wouldn't it?" She did not seem appropriately alarmed by this prospect. "Oh! And you should play croquet at your party, don't you think—wouldn't that be wonderful? Do you think you could get hold of some flamingos?" Alice asked thoughtfully. "Perhaps we could give them some sleeping tonic to calm them down."

Tilly looked at her in horror. "Are you joking?"

"No, I think it's an excellent idea. I daresay the flamingos would enjoy it more."

"You have a very unusual perspective on the world," Tilly said.

"Depends whose you are comparing it to," Alice said sagely.

33

A Whole Extra Character

Tilly headed back downstairs to find Oskar laughing with Jack as he cut out intricate flowers and vines from colored paper and Grandma spoke to someone on the phone behind the till.

"Everything okay?" he asked as Tilly sat down.

"We need to chat in a bit," she said vaguely. "You know, about the stuff we were talking about before." Oskar looked at her quizzically but nodded. At that moment Grandma came back over and put a gentle hand on Oskar's shoulder.

"It's your mum on the phone, Oskar. She wants a word. Nothing too serious, I don't—" But Oskar was already on his feet, heading to the till. "His *mamie* has to go into hospital for some tests," Grandma said to Jack and Tilly. "His father needs to look after her, so Mary's got to get the train over to pick up his sister. She's asked if Oskar can stay over here tonight, maybe tomorrow too, depending on whether she needs to help with anything in Paris. I'm guessing

Oskar's going to be feeling a bit delicate, though, so we'll need to all rally round and make sure he's doing okay."

Oskar came back to the table, looking a little wobbly. "Did Mum tell you?" he asked Grandma, who nodded.

"We're very happy that you're here, Oskar, even though it's in slightly sad circumstances, but it sounds like there's no need to worry, and they're just going to make sure everything's okay, as I'm sure your mum told you. It's just easier for your dad to have Emilie over here for a little bit. And we could certainly do with another pair of hands for the party tomorrow night—look how much you've helped already. Tilly, why don't you take Oskar upstairs and get the spare bed sorted for him?"

Tilly nodded and Oskar followed her out of the shop and upstairs.

"Are you okay?" she asked quietly. "I'm sure she's going to be fine."

"I guess," Oskar said. "I know she's going to be okay, I just wish I could have gone too. I don't really want to talk about it right now, though, if that's okay. What was it you wanted to say to me earlier?"

"Okay, well, let me know if you change your mind," Tilly said. "And what I needed to talk to you about was that yesterday, after you left, I went inside *A Little Princess* to try to see Captain Crewe . . ."

"You went bookwandering without me?" Oskar said, affronted.

"I didn't plan to," Tilly said. "I . . . I wanted to see my dad." The word still felt foreign on her tongue.

"What?"

"It's what I'm trying to tell you," Tilly said. "After you left, my grandparents told me the truth about who my father is."

Oskar's attention immediately snapped from being frustrated he'd missed a bookwandering opportunity to entirely focused on Tilly.

"The truth?"

"Well, what they said about him dying before I was born is true in some ways as he died in nineteen hundred and something. Inside a book."

"What?"

"My father is Captain Crewe."

Oskar looked baffled.

"From *A Little Princess*—he's the main character's dad and he dies."

"But . . . but how does that even work?" Oskar stuttered. "What does it mean?"

"Turns out no one knows. It's really not supposed to happen. My mum got into loads of trouble for falling in love with him. And it means I'm technically half-fictional, although I don't think there's an official word for it."

"And did you find him?" Oskar said. "When you went in? What was he like?"

"I saw him, but I didn't talk to him. But then it got even

weirder because when I tried to get back the last page of the book had been torn and I ended up in the Underlibrary," Tilly said as she found some clean sheets and towels and a new toothbrush. "And the other thing is that I found a copy of *A Little Princess* in Chalk's office that's different from mine, and from all the normal ones—I checked the copies in the shop."

"What were you doing in his office?" Oskar asked.

"I sort of broke in accidentally. He went mad when he found me," Tilly said.

Oskar looked at her in surprise. "I didn't think you were a breaking-into-offices-accidentally sort of person," he said as they dumped the stuff on the bed in the spare room and went back downstairs.

"Well, I didn't used to be the sort of person who leaped off the side of pirate ships either," Tilly replied.

"Fair enough," Oskar said. "There's definitely something off about that Chalk guy, though, right? He also seems to be super not into books for a librarian. I can't believe they let him work there. I wonder if he has other books that are different. Can you do the thing you did last time to magic us back there? How did that work?"

"I'm not sure," Tilly said nervously. "It's definitely not what's supposed to happen. I could try to do it again—but I didn't do it on purpose the first time so I don't know if it'll work. I think it must have something to do with the Endpapers Seb warned us about. When you let the book finish while you're still inside?"

"I suppose if you couldn't read the last line, that kind of makes sense," Oskar said slowly. "But didn't Seb say they were dangerous—and you just ended up back at the Underlibrary?"

"Yes, but . . . I wonder if it's because of who my dad is, because of how I'm, well, half-fictional. Do you remember that Seb said the Endpapers work as a kind of cushion to bounce characters back if something goes awry? And I guess I'm sort of half a character."

"That figures, I think."

"There was a bit when everything just went black, and cold, and I couldn't see anything, but it was like the blackness just went on forever . . ." Tilly said, shuddering at the memory.

"It doesn't sound like a fun place to get stuck," Oskar said. "And I guess Seb did tell us specifically not to go too near the end of a book. It's kind of risky just to look at some books, and didn't you say the differences between the normal copies and the one in Chalk's office were only small?"

"Yes, but why were there any differences? There's something strange going on. I wish I could just check," Tilly said, unable to ignore the niggling feeling in her brain. "And they weren't *that* small: there was a whole extra character."

"What did they do?" Oskar asked.

"Not much, really, but where did she come from?"

"Maybe it's just an old version," Oskar said, "and the writer changed his mind?"

"Her mind," Tilly corrected.

"Well, maybe she just changed her mind," Oskar repeated, "and took the character out?"

"But why would Chalk have it? It looked like a regular book and I'm sure that's not how it works, that you can have old copies of famous books with slightly different bits in. I suppose I should ask Grandad—maybe it's an Underlibrary thing."

"It's the sensible thing to do, I guess," Oskar agreed.

"Okay, it's decided," Tilly said, ignoring the slight sense of disappointment she was feeling. "I'll ask Grandad in the morning. I'm sure he'll know."

34

The Wrong Place at the Right Time

The next morning bloomed in a buzz of excitement about that evening's party. The family, plus Oskar, were sitting round the kitchen table, eating warm *pain au chocolat* when Jack arrived and started unloading all his paraphernalia. The shop was closed in preparation for the evening's party and he and Grandma planned to bake and decorate treats for most of the day. Oskar and Tilly were sent back out to the shop with Grandad to start carefully clearing the books from the display tables on the ground floor, which were being turned into a long tea party table.

As the three of them made piles of books ready to move upstairs Grandad hummed happily to himself, before Oskar elbowed Tilly in the side and gave her a look.

Tilly took a deep breath. "Grandad?"

"Yes, love?"

"Can I ask you something?"

"Of course," he said, still piling books up.

"When I ended up in the Underlibrary the other day Amelia said something to me about my mum . . ."

Grandad put his pile of books down and went to sit on the stairs, patting the step next to him for Tilly, as Oskar continued sorting books nearby.

"She said that after she'd had me," Tilly went on, "Mum tried to get into the Source Library, using your key, and that was part of the reason you'd retired early from being the Librarian."

"Well, yes, that's true, Tilly," Grandad said slowly. "Your mum got it into her head that she could somehow stop Captain Crewe from dying without leaving a trace in the Source Edition. She'd convinced herself that if she went with him once his story wasn't on the page, she'd be able to change the course of the story without altering Sara's. Of course, it wouldn't have worked—it doesn't bear thinking about what chaos she would have wreaked—but Mr. Chalk noticed her in there as soon as she entered, and she didn't have the chance to do any permanent damage before we found her."

"Was she trying to leave me?" Tilly asked quietly.

"Tilly, she wasn't thinking straight. It was a dangerous, reckless plan that I don't believe she'd thought through, but I am certain she wasn't trying to leave you. I think that she must have been either testing out whether she could do it with a view to coming back to collect you or even exploring whether she could get him out of the book without drawing any attention to either of them."

"How do we know she's not there now?" Tilly said. "Maybe she found a way back?"

"There's no way she could possibly have got back into the Source Library without us noticing. Remember, we tried to stamp her to check," Grandad said.

"Is that why Mr. Chalk hates me so much—because of what Mum did?" Tilly asked.

"Mr. Chalk is no great fan of our family for many reasons," Grandad said. "And none of them are your fault. We never saw eye to eye when we worked together and Bea using my key to access the Sources was the final straw. He's convinced himself that I'm somehow still trying to undermine him even now that I have nothing to do with the Underlibrary—that's what he was accusing me of when he burst in here last weekend. He was claiming that Amelia and I were somehow in cahoots, which is sheer nonsense. He likes Amelia about as much as he does me; he had his eye on the Librarian job when I left—in fact, after the scandal, he was extremely insistent that I must be forced out, if I wasn't willing to retire."

"But why does he hate *everyone* so much?" Oskar said, no longer pretending that he wasn't listening to their conversation. "And how come he can even bookwander when he doesn't seem to like stories?"

"Well, we all have different relationships with books,"

Grandad said carefully. "Obviously Enoch has an important link to them otherwise he wouldn't be able to bookwander. And, as we told you, he's a very diligent watcher and incredibly attuned to disturbances in the Sources. He might not be a friendly or a kind man, but he's not an evil one. He's devoted his life to the Underlibrary, even if his methods are unorthodox."

"Talking of which, and just hypothetically speaking," Tilly said, trying to sound casual, "say Mr. Chalk had a book and it was slightly different from all the other versions of that book, what might that mean?"

Grandad raised an eyebrow. "Hypothetically speaking I would say that I would be concerned as to how you knew that, but also that it was nothing to be alarmed by. If you were to read a book that had someone wandering inside, you would see the results of them being there temporarily on the page until they left, but usually a wanderer will have the book with them. If it was a Library copy, it would not be unusual for a librarian to be on a monitored wander. Now. Do I need to be anxious about why you're asking that question?"

Tilly and Oskar both shook their heads vigorously and Grandad laughed gently and stood up. "You're worryingly like your mother, Tilly," he said affectionately. "Please be careful."

Oskar and Tilly stole a quiet moment to regroup when everyone took a coffee break.

"So, it was just a librarian in the book," Oskar said. "That's why it was different, and that's why it was so undramatic—she was buying cake, right?"

"Yep, it was just a woman buying cake—it barely said anything in the bit I read, just that it was cold and she was playing with her necklace, then she bought almond cakes . . ."

Oskar pointed at Tilly's neck and laughed. "She's rubbed off on you obviously!"

And Tilly realized she was messing with her bee necklace as she talked. She stopped and stared at Oskar.

"Oh my goodness, are you thinking what I'm thinking?"

"Uhhh, that you want some cake?" he tried hopefully.

"Oskar. Just suppose, for one minute, that that woman wasn't just a librarian. Just suppose that that woman was my mother," Tilly said, fizzing with excitement.

"No, no, no, Tilly," Oskar said urgently. "You've missed out, like, a million steps there to get to that conclusion. You can't go around thinking every random woman wearing a necklace is your mother—that's just not how it works."

"But it's not a random woman! She's in *A Little Princess*, where my father is! And she's not in any other editions!"

"But, Tilly, why would she be in a copy in Chalk's office? It doesn't make any sense at all, and your grandad just told you they didn't find her in any books. You're seeing her there because you want to see her there."

"Maybe," Tilly said, "but surely it's worth going to check? There's no harm in at least trying!"

"No harm in trying out a theory about just wandering off the edge of a book? No harm in sneaking into the Underlibrary without telling anyone? No harm in risking running into Chalk? And what about Amelia—how would you explain being in the wrong place *again* to her?"

"Well, you never know what you might find, being in the wrong place at the right time," Tilly said.

"Did you read that in a book? Oskar said.

Tilly grinned. "No, I made that one up myself. Anyway," she said more quietly, "I don't want to go on my own and I need someone, well, someone who's best-friend material to come with me."

"Well, I guess we could go while the party is happening . . . ?" Oskar said, relenting quickly, his cheeks a little pink.

"Exactly," Tilly said. "We could be there and back before anyone's even noticed we've gone . . ."

35

A Bookshop Is Like a Map of the World

At five o'clock the Pages & Co. extended family gathered for an early tea of sandwiches in the kitchen before Oskar was commandeered by Jack to help with final details for the party, and Tilly was sent upstairs to get changed. It wasn't fancy dress, but guests were very much encouraged to wear a nod to the year's theme. Tilly and Grandma had found a full-skirted blue dress that had a distinctly Alice-y feel. Tilly wondered what the real Alice would make of it as she refastened her golden bee necklace round her neck and headed downstairs.

The bookshop had been transformed. The central display tables had been cleared away and there was just one long table heaving under Jack's creations. Pretty, mismatched china tea sets and cake stands were piled with scones topped with cream and jam, macarons of every imaginable color, and tiny, frosted cupcakes topped with sparkles. There were elegant finger sandwiches, and miniature twirled pastries, and at the center of the table, a four-tier Victoria sponge cake was messily iced and heaped with fresh flowers and fruit.

Tilly could see Oskar laughing as he helped Jack drape strands of white fairy lights along the bookshelves, getting them both tangled up. Grandad was pinning intricately cut paper flowers in garlands around the room, and Grandma was filling mismatched bottles with fresh flowers. There was soft string music playing in the background, which was disrupted only by the occasional giggle, or by the clattering of an array of teapots being filled with different kinds of tea or brightly colored cocktails for the grown-ups.

Tilly stood in the middle of the shop floor as though she was at the center of a merry-go-round and let herself soak everything up. The only thing missing was her mum.

"Oh, Tilly, you look lovely!" her grandma said as she noticed her standing there. "What do you think of the shop?"

"I love it," Tilly whispered. "It looks perfect." The atmosphere

of the bookshop settled on her shoulders like an invisible protective cape. Jack came over, wearing a top hat tied with colorful scarves in a nod to the Mad Hatter. He pointed at Oskar, who had the four playing card suits painted on his cheeks.

"I did them with eyeliner and lipstick," Jack said proudly.

Guests soon started to trickle in and Oskar and Tilly were on duty, taking people's coats, which they then unceremoniously heaped into a pile in the stock cupboard. The bookshop was soon full of the noise of music, laughter, and glasses clinking. After an hour or so, Grandad clambered up onto a chair and chinked a cake fork against his glass.

"I just wanted to take a moment to say thank you to everyone for coming, and thank you to everyone who visits Pages & Co. and keeps us open and adventuring. Some people see a bookshop as an archive, or a shrine, or even a time machine. But I think a bookshop is like a map of the world. There are infinite paths you can take through it and none of them are right or wrong. Here in a bookshop we give readers landmarks to help them find their way, but every reader has to learn to set their own compass. So, a toast," he said, raising his glass and looking directly at Tilly. "To finding your own adventure." The crowd raised their glasses before erupting into cheers.

As the room refilled with noise Tilly and Oskar slipped

upstairs. Tilly had both her mum's copy of *A Little Princess* and a brand-new edition in a Pages & Co. tote bag ready to compare with Chalk's version.

"Okay, now which book should we use?" Tilly said, scanning the shelves. "*Alice*, because I've been there the most times?"

"It seems as safe a choice as any," Oskar said, and the two of them linked hands as Tilly read them into the final chapter.

The smell of burned marshmallows was much stronger this time, no longer smoky and tempting but acrid and sticky like they'd been left on the fire for too long. Tilly felt the flip of her stomach as the walls folded down around them, leaving them standing in a lovely, carefully manicured garden with a large white house visible up the hill. There was a stream babbling somewhere nearby and the garden was lined with blossom trees and rose bushes.

"Where's Alice? Can you see anyone at all?" Oskar whispered, sounding slightly panicked.

"No," Tilly said. "Maybe this was a bad idea after all."

"There she is!" Oskar shouted suddenly, pointing down the hill, and Tilly tried to calm her breathing. She followed the direction of his finger and saw Alice lying under a tree, apparently asleep in the lap of a girl who looked remarkably like her, only a little older.

"I guess that's her sister," she said. "This is the end of the book after all; this is when she wakes up and her sister says it was all a dream."

"Hang on," Oskar said, outraged. "*Alice in Wonderland* ends with it all being a dream? But Ms. Webber always tells us that it's lazy storytelling to have it end as a dream."

"Yeah, but then her sister has her own sort of dream, and talks about telling it as a story to her future children."

"It sounds weird," Oskar said.

"The whole book is weird," Tilly said. "That's why people like it."

They edged closer to the two girls, and watched as Alice's sister gently shook her awake, smiling.

"Wake up, Alice dear!" she said. "Why, what a long sleep you've had."

"Oh, I've had such a curious dream!" said Alice. They could hear her telling all her adventures in Wonderland, as her sister listened, entranced. As she finished, her sister kissed her on the top of her head.

"It *was* a curious dream, dear, certainly, but now run in to your tea; it's getting late." And Alice stood up and dashed off up the garden toward the house as her sister lay back on the grass and dozed off in the late-afternoon sun, thinking about the stories she'd just heard.

"Well, what do we do now?" Oskar said.

"We wait for the last page, I suppose," Tilly said nervously. They hovered close to Alice's sleeping sister. "It's nearly here."

"What do you think will happen?"

"I'm not sure—but I'm rapidly realizing that reading a book

and being inside one are rather different things, and that one is considerably more complicated than the other."

"I wonder if—" but Oskar was interrupted by everything suddenly going slightly out of focus. Tilly felt as though she had just stepped off a roller coaster and her head was still spinning. Oskar grabbed her hand as they struggled to stay upright.

Tilly took a sharp breath as a blurry, transparent version of Alice ran backward down the hill straight past them, before laying her head back in her sister's lap. At the same time her sister picked up a book, and a white rabbit in a waistcoat ran past them, similarly hazy at the edges.

"The story is happening all at once; it's like it's being rewound," Oskar whispered. "What do we do?"

"We wait," Tilly said. They held tightly onto each other's hands as the world around them sped up even MORE until all the colors blended into a faded rainbow and then turned abruptly to black.

"Are you there?" Tilly whispered into the darkness.

"Uh-huh," Oskar said. "Although I think I might be sick."

"Okay, let's see if this has worked," Tilly said, letting go of Oskar's hand and feeling for the walls. She followed them along and breathed a sigh of relief when she found a door and a light switch roughly where she expected them to be. She flicked the light on and they squinted in the sudden brightness. They were standing in the middle of the same room that Tilly had stumbled into two days earlier.

"We've done it," she said. "We're back at the Underlibrary. I wonder why we always end up in this room."

"Can you remember the way to Chalk's office?" Oskar whispered, and Tilly nodded and gestured along the corridor.

They jogged briskly until they came to Chalk's office door. It was shut, and no light came from inside. Tilly leaned an ear very, very gently against the wood and couldn't hear anything. Taking a deep breath, she clicked open the door and poked her head round before giving Oskar a silent thumbs-up, and slipping inside.

The office was as neat and bland as it had been the last time. Tilly went straight over to the only bookcase that didn't contain ledgers, running a finger down the spines and pulling out *A Little Princess*. She sat cross-legged on the floor and started flicking through, trying to find the changed passage. Oskar sat in Chalk's chair and put his feet up on the desk as he flicked through Chalk's diary.

Minutes later Tilly threw the book down on the floor in frustration.

"It's changed back," she said. "The bakery bit is exactly like it's supposed to be. I swear that it was different."

"Okay," Oskar said. "Maybe it's a different copy or something. Or the change was just something to do with Chalk's job. Are you sure?" He joined Tilly on the floor and the two of them pored over the three copies of the book. Tilly read Chalk's copy, hoping to notice something different, while Oskar checked the same passages in the other two copies of the book.

"Do you think we could get away with taking that one back with us?" Oskar asked.

"Chalk seems like the sort of person to notice something of his going missing," Tilly said, staring uncertainly at the book in her hands. "Oskar, I'm sorry. I think I was wrong. It must just have been a librarian after all; I'm sorry for dragging you back here when—"

"Shhh," Oskar said.

"Did you hear something?" Tilly said, panicking.

"No! Look!" Oskar said, jabbing a finger down.

"This bit with the . . ." He seized the book and looked back down at the page. "The Montmorencys? There's a woman wearing a necklace with a bee on it." Tilly grabbed the book back out of his hand. It was the chapter where the rich family who live across the square from Miss Minchin's school are heading out for a Christmas party. Tilly read the passage aloud.

"*Several of the Montmorencys were evidently going to a children's party, and just as Sara was about to pass the door, they were crossing the pavement to get into the carriage which was waiting for them. Veronica Eustacia and Rosalind Gladys, in white-lace frocks and lovely sashes, had just got in, and Guy Clarence, aged five, was following them. He was led by the hand by a woman who seemed to be the nanny, but who was dressed very finely and who wore a slim gold necklace with a bumblebee charm around her neck, which Sara could see glinting festively.*"

Tilly's face drained of color as she rifled through the new copy of the book just to be certain and found the right passage. She pointed at the page.

"Look. She's definitely an extra character. The family doesn't have a nanny!"

"But what does that mean?" Oskar said. "How can it be your mum, Tilly? What if it's just a weird coincidence? Maybe your mum had this necklace because she likes the book?"

"But Grandad said that she had tried to get back to my father!" Tilly said.

"Yes, but she couldn't be in Chalk's copy, could she? Your grandad said they checked all books," Oskar said, trying to remain logical.

"There's no harm in checking again, though, right?" Tilly said, looking hopefully at Oskar. "As we're here. There's definitely something weird going on."

"You mean wandering inside Chalk's book?" Oskar swallowed. "Wouldn't he know?"

"I don't see how. It's just a normal book, isn't it? And we'll have it with us inside. It's just like wandering inside any other book, and look," she said, turning to the last pages, "the last page is there so we can get back easily. If it's not her, we'll just—"

"Shhhh," Oskar interrupted again.

"What now?" Tilly said.

She was focused entirely on finding her mother now, and had almost forgotten where they were.

"Can you hear footsteps?" he said.

They looked at each other in horrified silence as the undeniable sound of tapping heels echoed outside.

"I guess that makes the decision easier," Oskar said, and held out his hand as Tilly started to read.

36

Be Brave and Be Kind

The air shimmered and Chalk's office tumbled down around them, into the ground. Tilly and Oskar shivered, realizing immediately how inadequately dressed they were for the biting wind of Victorian London. They were back in the square that Tilly had visited by herself a few days ago, but they were standing directly opposite Miss Minchin's school.

They could see Sara, looking much thinner and dirtier since Tilly had first met her, standing on the street, watching a family of richly dressed, happy-looking children clamber into a hansom cab. A little boy with rosy cheeks and dark curls was holding a smiling woman's hand. Tilly's heart felt as though it had stopped. It was her mum.

"It's her," she whispered, drinking in the first glimpse she'd ever had of her mum in the flesh.

"Are you sure?" Oskar said gently.

"She looks exactly like she did in the photo your mum gave

me—she doesn't even look much older. And I just know, Oskar. It's her."

Tilly threw the book to Oskar, pulled her bee necklace out of the top of her dress, and dashed across the road to where her mum was helping the little boy up the steps. As Tilly reached the curb, she slipped on the wet ground and fell forward onto her hands and knees. She heard the children gasp and then felt a steady hand grasp her by the elbow and help her up.

"All you all right, miss?" Tilly looked up into her mother's concerned face. She waited for Bea to recognize her, but she simply held Tilly's arm gently. "Did you bump your head, my love?"

The other children had gathered round, but Tilly barely noticed them.

"Mum?" Tilly whispered.

For a moment her mum's eyes glazed over, before she shook her head as if trying to get rid of a persistent wasp. She took a deep breath and smiled kindly. "I don't have any children, my dear. I'm the nanny and governess to these rascals." She smiled warmly at the little boy who was still hovering around.

"You're Beatrice, aren't you?" Tilly tried again desperately.

"Why, my name *is* Beatrice," she said, surprise written across her face. "How on earth did you know that? Did you overhear one of the children?"

"Look, Miss Bea," one of the girls said. "She's wearing a necklace just like yours!"

Tilly's hand instinctively went to her necklace, touching the thin gold chain.

"Goodness, where did you get that from?" her mum asked. "It's the mirror image of mine."

"You got yours from my father! From Captain Crewe! And you had another made for me when I was born. I promise."

At Captain Crewe's name Bea's eyes again went hazy, as if searching for the memory from the very back of her mind, but, again, it passed and she shook her head sadly.

"My dear, I think you must have had a nastier fall than we realized. Let me take you to Miss Minchin's where you can lie down and I will come and see how you're doing after I've taken the children to their party. I will only be half an hour." She paused and turned to the oldest girl. "Janet, would you mind the others getting into the cab while I take this poor child across the square?"

"Of course, Miss Bea," the girl said, guiding the little boy carefully back toward the steps of the cab.

"I'm really fine," Tilly protested, panicking that she might be separated from her mother before she'd even had a chance to explain. "I don't need a lie-down." She looked over her shoulder, trying to spot Oskar, who was hovering on the other side of the street, unsure of how to help.

"I think you need a rest and a glass of water somewhere warm," Bea said. "Where on earth is your coat? Do you know where your parents are?"

At the last question Tilly started to cry.

"Oh, come now, my dear; it's not so bad. We'll find them and all will be well."

Putting her arm gently round Tilly's shoulders, Bea guided her to the door of Miss Minchin's school and knocked firmly. The door was opened by a pale-faced maid.

"May I speak with Miss Minchin, please?" Bea said. "This poor girl has had a nasty fall and needs to warm up. Perhaps Miss Minchin could spare some hot food and let her rest for a little while until we can help to locate her family?"

The maid led them silently into a stiflingly hot parlor, where pinch-faced Miss Minchin sat, looking imperiously over her half-moon glasses. Bea repeated the story and explained that she had to return and look after the children.

Miss Minchin gave a polite smile and nod. "Of course. Any friend of the Carmichaels is a friend of mine."

"What? Aren't they called the Montmorencys?" Tilly said, confused.

"I think she might have had a bit of a bang to the head. I'll pop back very soon, I promise. Thank you for your hospitality, Miss Minchin." Bea gave Tilly a warm hug and headed for the door.

"What did you say your name was, child?" Miss Minchin said.

"Matilda. Matilda Pages."

The name made Bea stop with her hand on the doorknob, as if she had heard the murmur of a song she once knew, but after a beat she opened the door and left.

As soon as Bea had gone the cold smile on Miss Minchin's face entirely vanished. "Who are your parents, Matilda? Why were you careening around the streets with no coat on, toppling into good families such as the Carmichaels?"

Tilly knew she certainly couldn't tell Miss Minchin the truth, so she gave her grandparents' names.

"Elsie and Archibald Pages," she said quietly, brushing away a stray tear from her face.

"I've never heard of them. Where do they live?" Miss Minchin said sternly.

"North London," Tilly said tentatively, not entirely sure where she was in London herself. Miss Minchin grimaced. "Thank you for having me, but I really don't need to stay here," Tilly insisted, struggling to be polite as she remembered the horrible way Miss Minchin treated Sara in the book.

"Believe me, child, I have no desire to keep you here either, but I cannot simply turn you out onto the street when the Carmichaels' nanny will be returning to check on your health at any moment. Becky and Sara will keep an eye on you." She rang a dainty silver bell on her desk and Becky, the girl Tilly had met in the corridor of the school on her last visit, skidded into the room.

"Stop gawping, Becky! This is Matilda. She has had a fall. Would you clean her scraped knees, please, and find her somewhere to sit in the attic while we wait for someone to retrieve her? Fetch her a glass of water, and some bread if there is any to be spared."

Becky nodded mutely.

"Well, go on then," Miss Minchin scolded. "I am grossly overworked and this school does not run on kindness and charity, although heaven knows I would be rich if it did."

Tilly stood up silently and followed Becky out of the parlor.

"I'll take you up to Miss Sara's room," Becky offered nervously.

"Her father died, didn't he?" Tilly said bluntly.

"Why, yes. Did Miss Minchin tell you? She has to live up in the attic with me now, and help with the teaching and looking after the little ones, as well as all the shopping and cleaning and fetching."

Tilly followed Becky up two steep flights of stairs; the first was covered by the same opulent carpet that was in Miss Minchin's parlor; the second was much narrower and darker, with only a threadbare carpet underfoot. At the top of the stairs Becky pushed open a wooden door to reveal a whitewashed room with a slanting roof and very little furniture.

"This is Miss Sara's room. I'm sure she won't mind you sitting in here for a little bit while she's out running errands." Becky shepherded Tilly to an old iron bed with a very thin-looking blanket on top. "I'm sorry it ain't warmer. I'll get you some water and see if cook will let me have some bread for you." She gave Tilly a small smile and closed the door behind her.

Tilly slumped back on the cold, hard bed and fought to keep more tears from coming. She knew she needed to get out of the attic, and the school, find Oskar, and get back to Pages & Co., but the thought of having to leave behind her mum, who did not even recognize her, felt too much to bear.

The sound of something being thrown at the glass skylight above her head forced her out of her melancholy. She climbed up onto a rickety-looking table under the skylight and heaved it open. Her head emerged into a different land above the rooftops of London. Brick chimneys and slate roofs were laced with curling smoke, and birds darted through the higgledy-piggledy maze of mismatched buildings. Tilly could even see the familiar dome of St. Paul's Cathedral half hidden in the smog. Something about the glimpse of a building that was present in her London too gave her a rush of determination just as a tiny stone hit her on the head.

"Ow," she muttered under her breath.

"Tilly!" yelled a very familiar voice. She twisted to look round and saw Oskar's head sticking out of a skylight in the house next door.

"What are you doing?" she called across. "How did you get in there?"

"It was empty!" Oskar shouted. "I tried ringing the bell of the school, but that grumpy maid wouldn't let me in, so I tried next door. When I knocked, the door just swung open. No one lives here! Come on then!"

"What do you mean, come on?" Tilly shouted.

"Climb across!" Oskar shouted. "Look, the roof's really flat, you'll be fine."

"You want me to climb across?" Tilly said in horror, looking down at the street far below, slick with rain. "I'll fall! You know if I die in this book, it's real, right?"

"Have you got a better plan?" he asked. "Come on. I can grab you when you're close. We need to get home before anyone notices, or before Chalk realizes where we are."

Tilly took a deep breath and started pulling herself up through the window by her arms.

"Excuse me, but who are you, and where are you going out of my window?" a polite voice said behind her, causing Tilly to jump and bang her head on the window frame. "Oh, I'm so sorry. I didn't mean to startle you."

Tilly dropped back down onto the table and turned to see Sara, her half-sister, standing in her threadbare dress, damp from the drizzle outside.

"I'm Matilda," she said, not at all sure how to explain herself. "I fell over outside the school and my . . . and the nanny of the family across the square brought me here. I think she thought a school might be a slightly more welcoming place than it is . . ."

"Oh! The Large Family! That is what I call them as there are so many of them. They always seem so happy and rosy and content, don't you think? It doesn't surprise me at all that they have employed a thoughtful nanny, even if she was misguided in believing Miss Minchin to be a charitable woman. You mustn't think me silly, but I like to imagine their names when I see them. I call the baby girls Ethelberta Beauchamp Montmorency

and Violet Cholmondeley Montmorency. I suppose it *is* rather silly when I say it out loud, but telling myself stories is the way I cope with living up in this lonely, cold attic, you see. Everything is a story, really."

"I don't think it's silly at all," Tilly said.

"So why are you trying to escape? I realize that this room is hardly welcoming, but I am sure Miss Minchin would let you leave."

"She says I have to stay until the nanny returns so she makes a good impression on the family," Tilly explained.

"That sounds very much like her," Sara said sadly. "Is it urgent that you get away now?"

"It is rather," Tilly said. "My friend is waiting for me, and we have ended up quite a long way from home. The reason we came turned out to be for nothing anyway."

"Shall we see what is to be done then?" Sara said, clambering back onto the table and popping her head out of the window.

Tilly climbed up next to her to see Oskar's mouth form a surprised "o." "This is Sara," she explained.

Oskar gave her an awkward wave.

"Let me give you a hand up," Sara said, cupping her thin hands so Tilly could get out onto the roof.

Tilly tentatively stepped up, feeling Sara's arms shake with the effort. She held on to the window ledge incredibly tightly and perched on the edge, testing how stable the roof slates were with a toe.

"I think you should just run really fast and not look down," Oskar said. "Or maybe just go very slowly and carefully?"

Tilly started to feel a little sick.

"If it were me," Sara said quietly from Tilly's side, "I would concentrate steadfastly on the friend you are trying to reach, and trust the path your feet set you on. 'Be brave and be kind, Sara.' That's what my father always told me."

"Your father told you that? My grandparents say something very similar," Tilly said, feeling electricity pass between them as Sara held her hand. Tilly gingerly got to her feet and found her balance.

Sara nodded, gave Tilly's hand a final squeeze, and let go. "It's always served me well if I'm in a tight spot. Good luck, Matilda."

Tilly took a deep breath and, one step at a time, edged along the slate roof separating her from Oskar. It was only a short distance, but the drop was high and the roof was steep. The slates were wet from the drizzle and she had very little to hold on to. She focused entirely on the window where Oskar was waiting, hands outstretched ready to pull her to safety, and tried not to let the memory of her mum cloud her mind. She froze as a slate came loose under her shoe and slithered down the roof and off the edge. Oskar winced as they heard it crack on the pavement far beneath them.

"Keep looking forward!" Oskar shouted, and she took a deep breath and another step toward him.

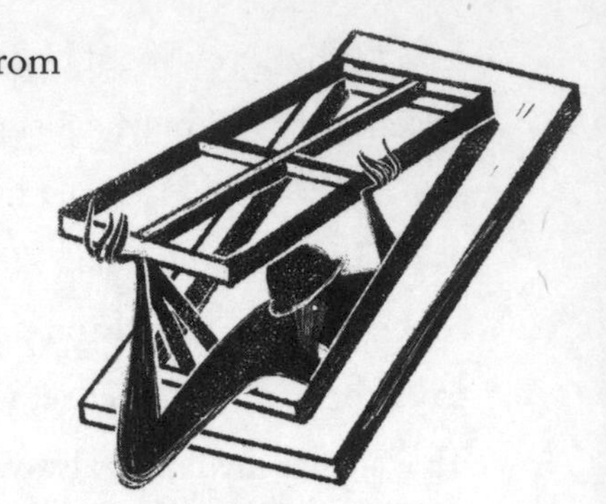

Tilly was only a little way from the window when she heard a yelp from Sara. She turned carefully to look over her shoulder and, to her horror, saw Enoch Chalk emerging from Sara's window, his face white with anger.

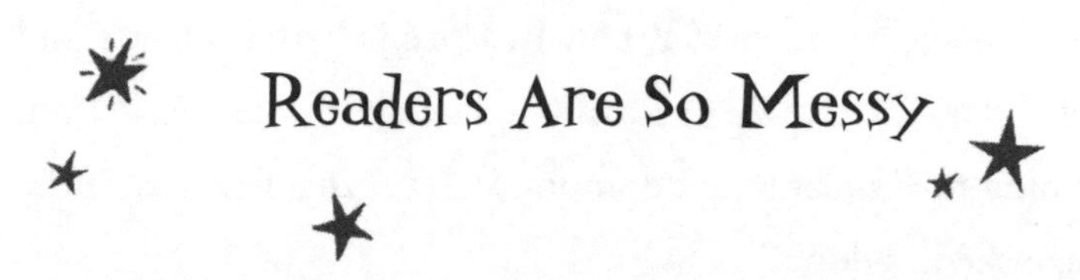

37

Readers Are So Messy

Tilly froze. "What are you doing here?" she asked.

"The question, Matilda, is what are *you* doing wandering in my personal library?" Chalk said, his voice full of ice.

"My mum is in here," Tilly said. "Why is my mum in one of your books?"

"Have you found your mother, Matilda? Will you be taking her home? Did she even recognize her own daughter? She's been here a long time, Matilda; her former life is a mere shadow now," Chalk gloated.

"You're supposed to be a librarian," Tilly said in confusion. "You're supposed to protect readers."

"That is where you are wrong," Chalk said. "I care very little for readers; they are so messy and yet so predictable all at the same time."

"But you work at the Underlibrary!" Tilly said.

"Yes, and I uphold the Underlibrary's rules. Rules your mother disobeyed. Not just disobeyed, but flagrantly flouted, in fact. Not only did she fall in love with a fictional character but she also attempted to access the Source Library and permanently damage a Source Edition. Beatrice is better off safe and out of the way here, where I can keep an eye on her. And I am beginning to suspect that I do not even realize a fraction of the damage she has done."

"You mean, you put her in here? You're keeping her here?" Tilly said in horror.

"Why, yes, of course. I thought you had worked that out already. You're clearly not quite as bright as you'd like to think, a trait that seems to run in your family."

"But how?" Tilly said.

"So many questions for one in such a precarious situation," Chalk said. "Enough chatter. I will need to find somewhere to keep you and the boy out of trouble for the foreseeable future—can't have you reporting back to Ms. Whisper or your dear grandfather."

His words shocked Tilly into action and she started scrambling across the roof. Oskar grabbed her outstretched hands as soon as he could reach and yanked her through the window, ripping her dress on the splintered frame as she toppled in.

"We need to get out of here, and fast," said Oskar. "We have to get back to Pages & Co. Now."

"I can't leave without my mum."

"You have to, Tilly," Oskar said. "When we're back and safe we can tell your grandparents, and they'll tell Amelia, and everything will get sorted out. But we have to leave. Where's the book?" Oskar said, increasingly panicked.

"I don't have it!" Tilly protested. "I gave it to you when I went to talk to my mum in the square. Didn't I?"

They looked at each other in horror.

"Is it still down there?" Tilly said weakly.

Oskar grabbed Tilly by the wrist and dragged her toward the stairs. "We just have to get to it before Chalk does."

They pelted downstairs and spilled out onto the street only to see Bea climbing the front steps to Miss Minchin's front door to check on Tilly.

"Tilly, we don't have time," Oskar said urgently.

"I'm sorry, I have to try once more," Tilly said, pulling away. "Get the book ready to go."

She ran up behind her mum, who turned at the sound of footsteps behind her.

"Oh, hello, my love. You're obviously feeling much better! Did Miss Minchin manage to track down your parents? I see she wasn't able to find you something warmer to wear," Bea said, frowning.

"I need you to come with me," Tilly said desperately. "Please, I can explain later."

"Try to calm down, Matilda. Can you explain to me what's going on? Are you safe?"

"You have to come with me; neither of us is safe," Tilly said, taking hold of Bea's hand. At that moment Chalk crashed out of the house only meters away from them. He stopped abruptly on the steps as he considered the scene in front of him, taking in Tilly tugging on Bea's arm and Oskar flipping frantically through the pages of the book. Chalk seemed to smirk to himself as if something had clicked into place in his brain.

At the sight of Chalk, Bea blanched. "Where do I know that man from?" she said under her breath, backing away. "Do you know him, Matilda?"

"Yes!" Tilly shouted. "All of this is his fault, and we need to go. You have to come with me."

Bea let herself be pulled toward Oskar, who was desperately smoothing out the final pages of the book as he ran toward his friend. He grabbed her and shoved the book at Tilly, who kept a tight hold of Bea with her other hand and started to read.

"No!" roared Chalk, and he lurched toward them as the damp streets of London started to fold down, and then they were standing, breathing heavily and damp from the drizzle, back in Chalk's office in the Underlibrary. As soon as the room became solid around them Bea slumped down against the wall in a faint.

Tilly desperately shook her mum's hand, trying to revive her so they could work out how to get back home, but the air shimmered again only moments later.

"First things first," a familiar cold voice said. "That book does not belong to you." And before Tilly could stop him Chalk snatched it from her.

"I knew you couldn't be trusted the first time I laid eyes on you, Matilda. You're just like your mother, and your grandparents—no respect for rules. And, even worse than them, I am coming to suspect that you should not even exist at all. Your family has always thought you were above the rest of us, that your self-righteous moral compass was more important than the laws laid down by people who know much better than you, always spurred on by some crooked perspective on right and wrong. Who decides what's right and wrong anyway?"

Tilly and Oskar stared at him as he raved, spit flying from his mouth.

"I . . . I don't understand," Tilly stammered. "What do you want?"

"A life! The freedom to make my own choices and my own destiny," Chalk said. "The things you take for granted and squander every single day!"

"But what's stopping you having that?" Tilly asked. "And what's it got to do with us?"

"Do you know, Matilda, the thing is, it didn't really need to be anything to do with you at all. If it wasn't for your mother sticking her nose where it wasn't wanted, we might never have got to this point."

"Matilda?" a shaky voice said from behind them as Bea pulled herself to her feet. Tilly, Oskar, and Chalk whirled round to see her gritting her teeth as she struggled to stay standing while trying to figure out exactly what was going on. She took a deep breath, gave Tilly a reassuring if tearful smile that seemed to say *just hang on a little bit longer*, before steeling herself and turning to Chalk.

"Now, Enoch, it's only fair to tell them the whole story, don't you think? A life is the last thing I take for granted," she said, her voice stronger now. "I sacrificed more than you could ever know to ensure that Matilda had hers to live to its fullest. To have the choices and freedom she deserves. The choices and freedom you feel you have been robbed of. And how dare you lecture us on right and wrong and breaking rules?

"You see, Matilda, my darling girl," Bea said, maintaining her defiant eye contact with Chalk. "That man has no more right to live in the real world than any other character. The truth is that Enoch Chalk is *entirely* fictional."

38

Some Books Are Loved and Some Are Forgotten

Chalk looked furiously at Bea. "You meddling, prying woman," he breathed. "You brought this all on yourself, you know. I tried to help you."

"You're still pretending that's the case?" Bea said coldly.

"You should have told me what your father was up to when you had the chance," Chalk spat.

"As I told you at the time, Enoch, there was nothing to tell! And, even if there had been, we both know you wouldn't—and couldn't—have given Ralph Crewe back to me," Bea said. "Not without damaging everything the Underlibrary stands for and protects."

Chalk sniffed. "And suddenly you care about that?"

"I have always cared about it, whether you believe it or not; I just care about my family more. And your slippery promises backfired, didn't they, when I learned your secret and you had to hide me away to protect yourself?"

"Enough of this," Chalk snapped. "You're going straight back where you belong now, and I'll even do you the courtesy of letting you keep your daughter and her friend, however he got mixed up with this debacle, with you. You can have your big reunion back in there," he said, brandishing his copy of *A Little Princess*.

"Uh, sorry to interrupt," Oskar said, putting his hand up to stall Chalk, "but can we just revisit the whole thing about you being fictional? Why do you even want to be here in the world and work at the Underlibrary?"

Chalk grimaced. "Readers are so fickle. They rally round the most undeserving of characters and cheer at the demise of the most admirable of men. It is not fair that some books are loved and some are forgotten, and it is not fair that I am vanquished on page 248 every single time. When the opportunity to escape presented itself I merely took advantage of it."

"But how?" Tilly asked. "We were told that was impossible! And how does no one here notice that you're from a book?"

Chalk flushed a deep scarlet. "My story attracts only the more discerning reader."

"You mean . . . no one reads your book?" Oskar said in disbelief.

"One reader, Mr. Roux," Chalk hissed, slamming his hand onto the desk. "I had *one* reader. I am entirely and completely out of print, so the copy from the Source Library is the only one containing my story. My predecessor as Reference Librarian was a weak man, but he served his purpose and allowed me to wander out of the pages of my book. He should have known better. There's a reason the Source characters are so well protected here: we have a level of agency and power that an ordinary character can only dream of. And once I was out, and had a taste of what this world had to offer, I simply made up my mind to stay. And so I sent him to one of my copies of a particularly bleak Charles Dickens novel to keep him out of the way. I imagine he is dead now," Chalk said casually. "It has been nearly twenty-five years, and Dickens characters do not tend to last long, especially spineless ones."

"Twenty-five years?" Oskar repeated in disbelief. "How old are you?"

"My author didn't have the depth of feeling to give me an age, but whatever age I am," Chalk said, "I have been for twenty-five years. I cannot age within the non-book world."

"Why hasn't anyone noticed you not changing?" Tilly asked.

"People rarely notice much outside their own heads; humans are infinitely self-occupied. They also have a staggering capacity to internalize whatever is presented to them, even Librarians, who claim to have an imagination. Besides, I am owed infinite lifetimes of freedom and opportunity."

"But you know you can never truly have the life you're chasing," Bea said. "You can only wander in books and the bookshops and libraries they give you access to."

"I thought characters couldn't wander in other books," Tilly said.

"Source characters can," Bea explained, a look of wonder on her face as she drank in the fiercely defiant eleven-year-old girl standing in front of her. "There are several things they can do that others can't; it's why the Source Library has such restricted access."

"Now is not the time to rectify your shamefully shallow understanding of the purpose of the Underlibrary," Chalk said. "And I assure you, Beatrice, a limited freedom here is a far more tempting proposition than being trapped in the place I was—a place where I was forced to live out what my creator planned for me endlessly with no way to change my own story, and no readers to give my story color or importance. You would not understand what freedom is," he said. "You are given so much and you waste it. And you bookwanderers are the worst of all, taking for granted not only the freedom of this world but infinite fictional ones as well. You are so greedy and so ungrateful."

"But what's the point?" Oskar asked. "What do you do other than fill in ledgers and tell people off for not following rules?"

"Now, Oskar," Chalk said, laughing without mirth, "I have read enough books to know that it is foolhardy in the extreme to reveal my plans to those who might wish to stop me. But let it be enough to say that the more flexible the boundaries between real life and books, the more problems there are for me. Now,

I have entertained your tedious questions for far too long and we all have places to be, some more permanent than others." With that he picked up his copy of *A Little Princess* and opened its pages.

In desperation Oskar darted forward and slapped the book out of Chalk's hand and onto the floor.

Everyone looked at Oskar in surprise and there was a moment's pause before Chalk, Tilly, and Oskar all dived to try to be the first to get hold of the book. In the tumult Oskar was pushed into one of the bookshelves, sending an avalanche of heavy green ledgers sliding to the floor with an almighty crash.

A few moments later the door flew open to reveal Amelia standing in the doorway.

"What on earth is going on here, Enoch?" she said, but words failed her as she spotted Tilly and Oskar squashed into one corner, before noticing who was leaning shakily, white-faced, against Chalk's desk.

"Bea? Is that really you?" she said in disbelief.

Bea smiled wanly. "Amelia."

"Ms. Whisper," Chalk said. "All my loose ends in one room—how convenient."

"What on earth is Beatrice Pages doing here? And Tilly and Oskar too?" Amelia asked. "Enoch, I think I'm going to need you to come with me."

"I'm afraid that's not an option," Chalk said, slowly getting up from the floor and edging backward away from the door.

"Enoch. Come with me now!" Amelia said more forcefully, shepherding Tilly and Oskar behind her as she spoke.

"I hate to repeat myself, Ms. Whisper, but that is not going to happen." His mouth quirked into a tight smile as he closed his eyes and dissolved into nothing right in front of them, leaving Amelia, Tilly, and Oskar alone in his office, all staring at Bea.

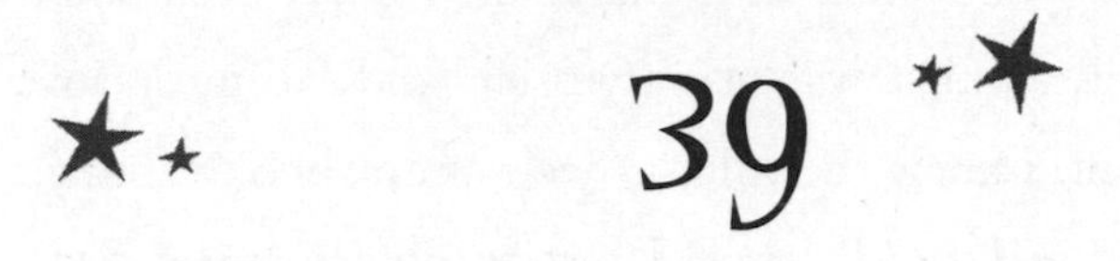

39

How the Story Had to End

"Matilda," Bea said, choking, her eyes filling with tears. "I still can't believe it's really you."

Tilly couldn't look at her mother. "You didn't recognize me," she whispered.

"I am so sorry," Bea said, her voice shaking. "I was not myself in there, only a shadow really. That book . . . I don't even know what Chalk or your grandparents have told you about it."

"A bit," Tilly said, glancing nervously at Amelia.

"It's all right, Tilly," said Amelia. "Your mum and I are old friends. I didn't know for certain, but I'd long had my suspicions about who your father is. I know it as a friend, not the Librarian, and I will keep it close, I promise you both."

Bea grasped Amelia's hand and squeezed it gratefully as she continued her story.

"Matilda, I promise you that when I first met your father I didn't mean to fall in love with him. It was a book I had enjoyed as a child. I loved it for the same reasons as you; I was barely aware of your father as a character. I never even bookwandered inside until I was at university, and falling in love was an accident. I knew the rules as well as any bookwanderer when I visited *A Little Princess*. I just wanted to meet Sara, really.

"The first time that he and Sara went to the school I was on the street, just watching. But when they left I was standing too close and the horse took fright when it saw me, and nearly kicked me. Ralph jumped out immediately to make sure I was okay, and everything just snowballed and I couldn't stop it, even though I knew how the story had to end.

"I knew I should go back, but I couldn't bear to leave him. It wasn't until I realized I was expecting you that I knew I had to come home—I couldn't risk having you inside the book. The only way to guarantee your safety was for you to be born in the real world. And then, afterward, I was desperate to find a way for us all to be together, but it wasn't possible. I tried to see him. I wanted to tell him about you, but it never worked how I planned it: the horse didn't take fright, or your father didn't notice, or I just wasn't in quite the right place at the right time, and he and Sara always left without seeing me. In the end I didn't know what to do. I just wanted you to know your father. And I wanted him to know you.

"And then, while I was in the Underlibrary with your grandad, helping him clear out his office, Chalk took me to one side without warning and told me that he knew of a way that Crewe and I could be together in the real world. Chalk knew nothing about you, Tilly, but he did know how desperate I was—everyone did after the Source Library debacle. He said he could help me if I told him what Dad was doing to stop his plans."

Tilly looked confused. "What plans? And what was Grandad doing?"

"That's the thing, Tilly," Bea said. "I don't think Grandad knows anything about Chalk being fictional, or any plans. He certainly never spoke to me about it."

"As far as I'm aware Archie knows nothing about Chalk's true identity," Amelia said quietly.

"But how do you?" Tilly asked. "And why did you let him keep working here?"

"I've suspected for a while that something was awry, but I didn't know for certain until tonight," she said. "And I wanted him close by while I tried to find evidence and work out what he was trying to achieve. But I think that might be a story for another day."

"But how did *you* find out that he's a character from a book?" Tilly turned back to Bea.

"Completely by accident," Bea said. "When I came to meet him to find out more about what he was offering, I hadn't told your grandparents where I was going—I couldn't tell them I was trying to find another way for us to be with your father. When I arrived he wasn't in his office so I just went in and waited and absentmindedly flicked through the book on his desk as I didn't recognize the title."

"Like mother like daughter, am I right?" Oskar said, but no one laughed.

"It was stamped as a Source Edition," Bea continued, "so it shouldn't have been in here anyway. There were so many blank pages with only the odd page or paragraph printed here and there. But my eye was caught by the name Enoch Chalk, and as I flicked through, it kept coming up.

"I hadn't even joined the dots in my own brain when he stalked into the room and saw me reading his book. He started yelling at me, telling me no one could know, that it was a secret. He started ranting about how only a handful of people had noticed anything wrong over the years, and that they had all been dealt with.

"Then it dawned on me. Why he was so angry and terrified. I realized it was him in the book. His name being the same wasn't a coincidence, and it wasn't from him having traveled in as a bookwanderer. I went for the door, but he wouldn't let me leave, just grabbed my wrist, closed his eyes, and the next thing I knew I was inside *A Little Princess*. He let go of me and vanished, and I was stuck, because he hadn't even brought the book with us, let alone left it with me. And I would have been there for who knows how long if you hadn't found me, Matilda."

"And Oskar," Tilly said quietly.

"But why didn't you get stuck in the Endpapers?" Oskar asked Bea.

Amelia looked at Tilly, Oskar, and Bea and sighed deeply. "Chalk seems to have created some sort of loop, and even books that can't be stamped. There's obviously an awful lot more explaining that needs to be done, but I think perhaps the priority right now is to get you all home." She helped Bea out of her chair and wrapped her friend up in a warm hug. Tilly could see tears on both of their cheeks. "Tilly and Oskar, if we took a shortcut back to Pages & Co., do you think you could pretend to forget about it?"

They nodded and followed Amelia, who still had an arm round Bea, out of Chalk's office, back through the main library hall, and to the Map Room.

Tilly looked at Amelia in confusion.

"I know I showed you this room before, Tilly. But it has a rather less publicized function, only to be used in emergencies by the most senior and trusted of librarians." They followed Amelia in and she closed the door behind them. "Tilly, if you wouldn't mind, perhaps you could find Pages & Co. on the map again?"

Tilly found the tiny glowing light that marked home, and turned expectantly to Amelia.

"And next, if you could just pop your finger on that light? Don't worry, it's not hot. Now read the bookshop name?" Tilly did as she was asked, but nothing happened. "Perfect, thank you, Tilly. Now, Oskar, would you mind getting the door?"

"The door we just came in through?" Oskar said hesitantly.

"The very same," Amelia said, nodding her head toward it.

Oskar went back to the door and opened it. The doorway looked like it had a sheet of tissue paper hanging in front of it.

Amelia grinned at Tilly and Oskar. "Just between us, remember?" she said, and the four of them went through.

It was like walking through a waterfall made out of magic. There was a second when their vision was blurred and they couldn't see anything at all, and then they were in the main entrance to Pages & Co., with the party going on as if they had never left.

"I told you they wouldn't notice we'd gone," Tilly said.

"I'm glad to see this evening hasn't stopped you being annoying when you're right," Oskar said, but he was smiling.

The bookshop was full of people and light and music. Grandad was behind the till, putting a pile of books in the brown paper bags printed with the Pages & Co. logo for a customer holding a cocktail. He glanced up and saw the four of them looking a little shellshocked in the doorway. When he noticed who was being supported by Amelia he staggered a little on his feet. He left the customer mid-sentence and walked toward them.

"Is that you, my little Bea?" he said, holding out a hand toward Beatrice. Bea collapsed into his arms and they held on to each other for a very long time.

"I'll go and find your grandma," Amelia said, and soon Elsie joined her husband and daughter and pulled Tilly in.

Amelia put an arm round Oskar's shoulder. "Well done," she said. "I don't know all the details, but I do know that Tilly couldn't have done this without you."

Hours later, after all the guests had gone home, Grandad, Grandma, Bea, Tilly, Amelia, and Oskar were sitting on a blanket round a circle of candles and leftover cake. Tilly didn't quite know how to be around the mum she'd never known, but simply being next to her was a start, and every time Bea smiled at her she felt one of the tiny cracks in her heart start to knit back together, even if the edges were still a little messy.

Tilly and Oskar, mouths full of cake, explained exactly what had happened that evening, with Bea adding how she had discovered Chalk's secret and Amelia filling in any other gaps. When she said that Chalk had escaped Grandad gave a shudder.

"Do we have any idea where he's gone? I know you are more than capable of dealing with this, Amelia, but a Source character on the loose who seems determined to bend the rules of book-wandering to his own aims is a rather unprecedented turn of events, even for the Underlibrary."

"We've got some educated guesses about where to begin," Amelia said. "I've asked some colleagues to seal off his office, and we are going to start with the very small supply of books in there, and any books we know he has a historic link to. The rules of bookwandering are being stretched and tested in a way they haven't been before, maybe even beyond Chalk's meddling."

"You must let me know if I or Elsie, or Tilly and Oskar, can be of any help," said Grandad. And to one side Oskar choked a little on a mouthful of cake when he heard his name.

"I will, of course, Archie. We'll find him and deal with him," Amelia said, and Grandad nodded. "He may be a Source character, but they still have their limits.

"But, Tilly, I have one more question: how did you get back to the Underlibrary again without any of the librarians noticing? Did you use the damaged copy of *A Little Princess*?"

Tilly shook her head fiercely. "No, you said not to! We, uh, we sort of went via the Endpapers of *Alice in Wonderland*," Tilly confessed sheepishly. "I sort of put everything together—what Seb told us, and what happened when I ended up back at the Underlibrary when the last lines were missing from *A Little Princess*—and realized that I could travel from the Endpapers because of who my father is, and the whole being half-fictional thing."

"So we just traveled to the very end of the book and waited, and everything went all trippy and weird and sort of rewound around us," Oskar finished.

"That was incredibly risky," Amelia said, pale-faced. "I'm sure Seb warned you that the Endpapers are a dangerous place."

"But ingenious, you have to admit," Grandma said, failing to keep a distinct note of pride from her voice.

Amelia tutted, but with the hint of a smile on her face. "Honestly, Elsie."

"Speaking of the end of *Alice*," Tilly said, trying to change the subject a little, "why does Alice's story end with the whole thing being a dream?"

"Well," Grandad said, "I've always thought that it's because the writer is saying that our dreams and our stories matter. I think it's quite beautiful that you can read the whole book as Alice telling her sister a story. And then Alice's sister is thinking about passing on the story to their future children, because stories last much longer than we do. Our stories are how we will be remembered—so we've got to make sure they are worth telling."

Epilogue

"I think it's time," Bea said to Tilly, who nodded. It was a frosty weekend at the start of December and every day since she had come home Bea and Tilly had got to know each other a little better than they had the day before. Their relationship was still fragile, but it was beautiful and sweet like spun sugar.

Tilly got out her brand-new copy of *A Little Princess* and turned to the page where Captain Crewe and Sara first arrive at Miss Minchin's—the moment Bea had first met Captain Crewe, and the moment Tilly had first seen her father. They held hands and Tilly read them in.

Even as the smoggy Victorian square blossomed around them, they did not drop each other's hands. They watched as the black cab drew up to the school steps and a small girl with a black bob got out, clutching the hand of a tall man. The two characters climbed the steps to the school and rang the doorbell.

As the door opened Captain Crewe happened to glance behind him to where Bea and Tilly were standing. He tilted his head as if he recognized them but couldn't place from where, and then offered them a smile and a tip of his hat before disappearing inside. Bea pulled Tilly closer to her as she wiped a tear from her cheek. She took a deep breath and smiled, and Tilly read them back to Pages & Co., where Grandad had the kettle on.

Acknowledgments

To Mum and Dad, who gave me a childhood full of books and library visits, and taught me to love learning and words. To my sister, Hester, who I love fiercely, and who this book is for. To my grandparents; I borrowed bits of all of you to make Tilly's grandparents so special.

To all the Brays and Kitchens, and the Collier/Cotton family.

To my agent, Claire Wilson, who is a constant source of wisdom, encouragement, and kindness. To Rosie Price and Miriam Tobin, and everyone at RCW.

To the three editors of this book: Lizzie Clifford, who acquired it; Sarah Hughes, who tamed it; and Rachel Denwood, who helped it over the finishing line. To Jo-Anna Parkinson, Alex Cowan, Elisa Offord, Julia Sanderson, David McDougall, Elorine Grant, Francesca Lecchini-Lee, Beth Maher, Jessica Dean, Carla Alonzi, Ann-Janine Murtagh, and the whole team at HarperCollins Children's Books who have made this experience so wonderful. To Paola Escobar, for her beautiful illustrations.

To Katie Webber and Cat Doyle, for more things than I have space to list here.

To my friends: Kiran Millwood-Hargrave, Rosalind Jana, Kate Rundell, Tom de Freston, Kevin Tsang, Melinda Salisbury, Lizzie Preston, Amy Stutz, Erin Minogue, Jamie Wright, Jon Usher, Anne Miller, Sarah Shaffi, Sarah McKenna, Alice Ryan, Eric Anderson, Naomi Reed, Naomi Kent, Sarah Richards, Jo Kitchen, Laura Iredale, Jen Herlihy, Jennie Rickell, and Jules at the Aylmer Pantry, where I wrote and edited so much of this book.

To those who encouraged me at the earliest of stages: Alan Weir, Jacqueline Hughes-Williams, Cathy Rentzenbrink, and John Ironmonger.

To the literary world, online and in real life, including everyone I worked with at The Bookseller, who gave me a community of book-lovers and friends and like-minded people just when I needed it most. To Anne Shirley, Sara Crewe, and Alice, and also to Lyra Belacqua, who is sadly still in copyright.

And to Adam Collier, for everything, always.

she had lived a long, long time. At this moment she was remembering the voyage she h just made from B bay with her father,
Captain Crewe. Sh king p, of the Lascars
passing silently t on it, o playing about on the
hot deck, and of so ung offic used to try to make
her talk to them and laugh at the thi rincipally, she was
thinking of what a queer thing it was e time one was in
India in the blazing sun, and then in the middle e ocean, and
then driving in a strange vehicle through strange where the

that's
time
said the
tter's remark
nd yet it was
d you,' she
mouse is asleep
a little hot tea
its head impa-
pon its nose. eyes, 'Of course,
, and said, without opening
course; just what I was going to remark myself.'
'Have you guessed the riddle yet?' the Hatter said,
turning to Alice again. 'No, I give it up,' Alice replied:
'what's the answer?'
'I haven't the slightest idea,' said the Hatter. 'Nor I,'
said the March Hare.
Alice sighed wearily. 'I think you might do someth
tter with the time,' she said, 'than waste it in aski
t have no answers.' Time as
said the Hatter, 'you wouldn't tal
, it. It's him.'
't know what you mean,' said Alic
don't!' the Hatter said, tossing his
sly. 'I dare say you never even spo
'Perhaps not,' Alice cautiously repli
have to beat time when I learn musi
'Ah! that accounts for it,' said the H

shoulder with some curiosity
she remarked. 'It tells the da
doesn't tell what o'clock it is
'Why should it?' muttered t
watch tell you what year it i
'Of course not,' Alice repli
that's because it stays the sa
time together.'
'Which is just the case wit
Alice felt dreadfully puzzl
seemed to have no sort of
was certainly English. 'I do
she said, as politely as she
'The Dormouse is asleep
and he poured a little hot t
The Dormouse shook its
said, without opening its e
just what I was going to re

w'fly handsome, Anne. And he teases the
e. He just torments our lives out."
ked having her life tor-
said Anne. "Isn't his
the porch wall with Julia Bell's and a
n?"
er head, "but I'm sure he doesn't
I've heard him say he studied the
eckles."
s to me," implored Anne. "It isn't
But I do think that writing
t the boys and girls is the
ee anybody dare to write my
se," she hastened to add,
. She didn't want her name
ting to know that there
Diana, whose black eyes
voc with the hearts of
red on the porch walls in
nt as a joke. And don't

Crewe was only seven. The fact w wever,
was always dreaming and thinking gs
not herself remember any time when
thinking things about grown-up people and the
they belonged to. She felt as if she had lived a l
long time. At this moment she was remembering
voyage she had just made from Bombay with her
Captain Crewe. She was thinkin
Lascars passing sile
playin

he
nents
he
than not.
name that's
Julia Bell's and a
es," said Diana,
e he doesn't like Julia
rd him say he studied
y her freckles."
bout freckles to me," implored
any. But I
wall
"Oh, don should
Anne. "It isn't delicate when I
do think that writing take-notice up
about the boys and girls is the s
just like to see anybody dare to w
with a boy's. Not, of course," she hastened to add,
dy would." Anne sighed. She didn't want
But it was a little humiliating

slowly through the big thoroughfares.
She sat with her feet tucked under her, and lean st her
father, who held her in his arm, as she stared out window at
the passing people with a queer old-fashioned thoughtfulness in her
big eyes. She was such a little girl that one did not expect to see
such a look on her small face. It would have been an old look for a
child of twelve, and Sara Crewe was only seven. The fact was,
however, that she was always dreaming and thinking odd things and
could not herself remember any time when she had not been
thinking things about grown-up people and the world they
longed to. She felt as if she had lived a long, long time. At this
ment she was remembering the voyage she had just made from
bay with her father, Captain Crewe. She was thinking of the
of the Lascars passing silently to and fro on it, of the chi
g about on the hot deck, and of some young officers' wi
sed to try to make her talk to them and lau
. Principally, she was thinking of what
ne time one was in India in the blazi
f the ocean, and then driving in a str
treets where the day was as dark as the night. She
o puzzling that she moved closer to her father. "Papa